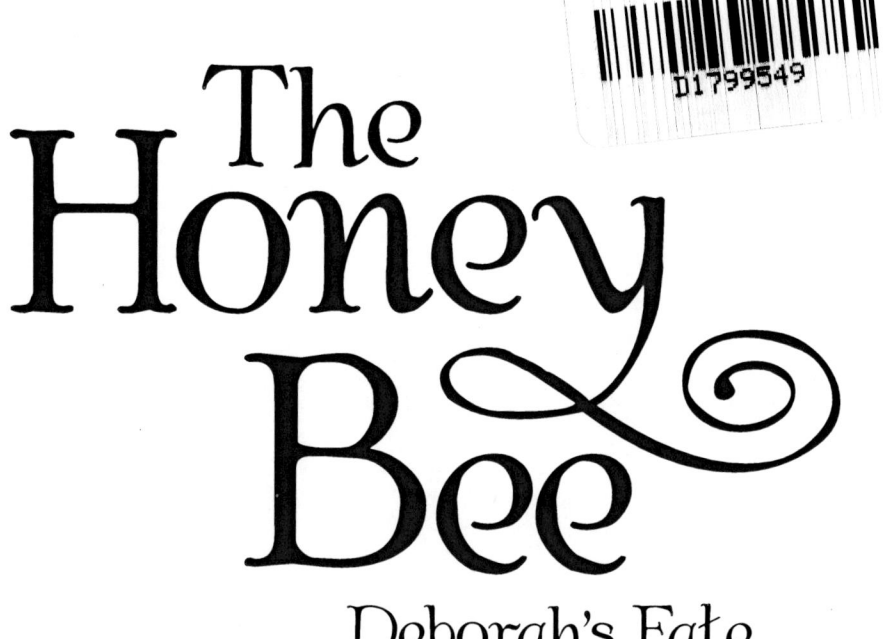

The Honey Bee

Deborah's Fate

A Novel

by

Heribert Breidenbach

authorHOUSE®

AuthorHouse™
1663 Liberty Drive
Bloomington, IN 47403
www.authorhouse.com
Phone: 1-800-839-8640

This book is a work of fiction and the names of all characters are fictional as is the name St. Francis Nursing Home.

Published by AuthorHouse 03/05/2015

ISBN: 978-1-4918-5439-6 (sc)
ISBN: 978-1-4918-5438-9 (hc)
ISBN: 978-1-4918-5437-2 (e)

Library of Congress Control Number: 2014901006

Print information available on the last page.

Any people depicted in stock imagery provided by Thinkstock are models, and such images are being used for illustrative purposes only. Certain stock imagery © Thinkstock.

This book is printed on acid-free paper.

Other works by the author:

A SONG FOR NATALIE   Scholarly articles on 17th century
A Holocaust Novella   literature.
Proctor Publications, 1995
Ann Arbor, Michigan

A quotable quote:

Mélissa, the honey bee, speaks:

"Our brains are no more than one fourth of a cubic millimeter in size. It would take about 700,000 bee brains to make one human brain. Humans, therefore, ought to be 700,000 times more intelligent than we are, but in the bee world we all know that they are not. In other words, a big brain is just a big brain, nothing more.

Characters

If you eat honey, my son,
and if the new honeycomb
is sweet to your taste,
then you will know
what wisdom is to your soul.
If you find it, you will have a future,
and your expectation
will not be cut off.

Proverbs, 24:13–14

Contents

Part I

I am all alone now, too tired to fly home with my last load of pollen and nectar, and none of my sisters knows where I am. It is so peaceful here, resting and dreaming embedded in this white rose. This is my first time in a rose. The gentle breeze, the sweet aroma, the rays of the evening sun filtering through the rose petals into my cone-shaped eyes, and the light blue sky flooding my ocelli, are all lulling me into tranquility.

I have labored all my life for my community, my family, 40 long days. How many are we? 10,000? 20,000? 30,000? I don't know. I was one of the fastest fliers, flipping my wings almost 250 times per second, and I flew as fast as 12 miles per hour. I gave it all I had, but now I feel no desire to leave this velvet rose. Where will the September winds carry my soul?

RUTH'S DILEMMA

"I am not going to let him do that, Mom, and I am not going to tell him where I hid it."

"Hid what, my dear?"

"His slingshot."

"Has Eric been aiming at birds again?"

"He missed a robin by one inch. Then I saw him aiming at a bee. She is sitting inside of a white rose, looks like she is taking a nap. She is so cute, golden brown with three stripes like grandpa's bees. He was aiming the slingshot at her when I grabbed it out of his hands. I am going to tell grandpa."

"Now don't be a tattle tale. Grandpa has more important things on his mind."

"I've got important things on my mind, too. Let's see if the mail has come."

"Angie, how many letters did you write today?" Ruth yelled as Angie was dashing out the front door.

"I only answered the five I received yesterday. One is from England."

"Angie, Angie, you are spending a fortune on postage stamps."

"I love getting letters, Mom."

★★★

Ruth was clipping roses while Angie was shut up in her room with her mail.

The next-door neighbor happened to walk by.

"Roses do well here in California, Mrs. Riley, from May until October.

"Hi Larry. My home is only half the size of yours. So I have to make up for it with roses."

"Your house may be small, but your rose trees flanking the walkway, and those climbing roses on both sides of your front door, and the trees with the yellow lemons on the manicured lawn make us neighbors feel we are living next to a fairytale land."

"Oh Larry, shut up! You are just being kind. You are trying to make me feel good because Travis left us. That damned alcohol! I feel like smashing every whisky bottle at the Starlight."

"And that dancer, I suppose."

"It seems that the whole street knows about it."

"There is a lot of gossiping."

"Then let me set the record straight. Travis took to the bottle after the cab company laid him off. He already drank too much before then but you could still call him a social drinker. Then disaster struck. He had been at a party too long before picking up two elderly ladies in his cab and promptly ran a red light. Tires screeching, horns tooting, missing a bus by one inch, one of the ladies on the back seat fainted. A cop on a motorcycle happened to be there and promptly ticketed him after smelling booze, and although Travis could not walk a straight line, he later tried to tell the judge that the reason for his distraction had been the constant chattering of the two old women on the back seat. The judge had to use all of his willpower not to burst out laughing and fined him $500. The following day the cab company fired Travis. After that he became a nightly fixture at the Starlight. You probably knew that already."

"I am afraid I did."

"Travis has always had a high opinion about himself. He felt that the available jobs in this town were below his dignity. The local elementary school was looking for a custodian. Two restaurants were looking for kitchen aids, dishwashers. He would not consider it. A month passed without income until my mother with her Irish temper gave him a piece of her mind for which he will never forgive her. Four more weeks passed until that day when he took off for Las Vegas, 'looking for greener pastures,' as he explained while kissing me good-bye. He was going to establish himself and get us out of this hut, he said."

"Well, maybe he meant it."

"That is what I believed until my dad made the time bomb explode. He had found out that Travis had taken the nightclub's striptease dancer with him. She is a redhead, redder than I. Her name is Isabel Macintosh. 'She is from New Orleans, and boy, can she dance!' dad told me. Here

I am. Angie is twelve. She keeps his photo on her dresser. Eric is eight. Travis taught him how to use a slingshot but not much else. He is Eric's hero."

"Ruth, I heard that there is no romance between him and the dancer, that he talked her into going with him so that he could open up his own bar with Isabel as the principal dancer."

Ruth dropped her clippers. The evening sun made her reddish-blond hair look like fire. She turned around and said: "Oh, yes? How come he never told me about that? It has been almost two months now, and he called me only a few times and only at the beginning. Each time he calls from a public phone, and when I write, his answers are short like: 'Don't worry! I cannot write now. I am very busy setting up the business.' He inquires about the children with just one brief sentence. I called Travis' parents in Los Angeles, Bill and Helen. They don't have his phone number either but they gave me his mailing address. My mother-in-law in Los Angeles had been under the impression that Travis and I had planned that together but could not understand one thing: 'Who is that woman with him?' she asked. She also told me that the two are sharing a one-bedroom apartment."

"You don't believe that."

After a pause Ruth answered: "I do." The veins on her temples began to swell, but then she changed the topic. "Angie has taken to letter writing. She has discovered the world of pen pals. Letters are all she thinks about. She writes to Travis every other day, now that we have his mailing address. Once a week he answers her, always saying the same thing: 'Thank you for your letter. I love you. Give my best to Eric.'"

"Ruth, he will be back and he will straighten out."

"Nope, I cannot compete with that nightclub dancer."

Two fiery redheads, Larry thought walking to his house next door. *They could set a gasoline truck on fire.*

★★★

Angie and Eric were in Angie's bedroom.

"Angie, I wish I had this picture of dad. He looks cool in his uniform."

"That was his Air Force uniform from the time he served in Korea. He is the best looking dad in California. I'll let you borrow the picture. The back of the photo has a date on it. It says *Korea, September 1952.* This is what dad looked like 17 years ago, when he was 25."

"How did you figure that?"

"Well, now is September 1969. From September 1952 to September 1969 it's 17 years. He was born in 1927. From 1927 to 1952 is 25 years."

"How do you know all that?"

"Girls are smart."

"Oh yeah? I bet you that you don't know how to aim with a slingshot. I can hit a small pebble stone on a pole 15 feet away."

"I firmly believe that."

"Why can't mom have a copy made by a photographer? It should be enlarged."

"Eric, that costs money. As a waitress at the diner mom is not making a lot of money. Some people don't even tip her."

"We will be rich, Angie. Dad is going to make a lot of money in Las Vegas."

"I am not so sure about that, but I tell you what: I'll let you keep the photo on your dresser if you will let me keep the slingshot."

"You are no fun. How come you get letters every day and I get none?"

"You never write. You are allergic to books, reading and writing. There comes mom."

"What are you two up to? Eric, have you done your homework?"

"Mom, I'll do it Sunday afternoon, promise."

"You know the rules, Eric. If you are not at your homework in five minutes, you will never see your slingshot again. Remember tomorrow is Saturday, grandpa's birthday. We are all going. He may need your help with the honey extracting. You can learn something and get a good foundation. Some day you might inherit his six beehives. I hope I did not buy that nice beekeeper's suit for nothing. Now get to your homework!"

Eric went to his room.

"Books! This English lesson is boring. Why do schoolbooks have to weigh a ton? Diagram sentences. I am going to diagram that bee. 'You can learn something and get a good foundation.' She is hiding my slingshot. Girls are mean. Bees are stupid. Books are boring. I feel like I am locked up. I have no freedom. I wish dad were here."

MÉLISSA

The velvet texture of these petals takes me back to my cell in the soft wax comb when I first became aware of myself, conscious of my existence. Was it the pressure of the six walls against my developed but tender body, the sweet aroma from the outside, or was it the buzzing all around me that made me break out of my confinement? I tasted freedom but now I am confined again. And yet, I feel so relieved, so free from life's burdens like cleaning cells, repairing and building new combs, carrying out the dead, feeding my roly-poly brothers, fanning cool air into the hive, defending the gate against intruders and, finally, flying out for miles, day after day, pollinating fruit trees for people who are not always very nice to us. ... The rays of the evening sun and the soft breeze are lulling me into a world of the unknown. Where will the evening winds carry my soul?

THE WALSHES

Fred and Mary Walsh and their daughter Deborah had just finished breakfast. Fred was stuffing his pipe with his favorite brand of tobacco, which Deborah had given him as a birthday present, even though gift giving had been scheduled for the afternoon.

"Fred, weren't you going to extract honey today?" asked Mary. "I am sure that Angie and Eric would like to help you on your birthday. Ruth went to the bee-keeping supply store and bought them special outfits."

"You don't say!"

"It is nine o'clock. They should arrive any minute."

"It is not exactly what I had planned for today, but okay. I only have two hives left to do. 40 frames, and with their help we can get it done this morning, including cleanup."

As Fred left the house, Mary muttered: "He is always so agreeable, even after 40 years. He and Deborah are one of a kind."

"What, Mom did you call me?" Deborah yelled from her bedroom.

"No, I was just talking to myself."

"But you were talking about me."

"Yes, my dear, but something nice. I was saying that you and dad are always so agreeable."

"That's nice to hear because people usually gossip behind my back."

"Debbie, you always tend to exaggerate," yelled Mary, not noticing that Deborah had already come out of her bedroom and was standing behind her.

"Well, why do I never get invited to any party? Why does no man ever ask me out? Because I limp and because my chin curves to the right and my nose isn't straight, and on top of it all, I am a hunchback."

"Hunchback? That is hardly noticeable. Your large hazelnut eyes, your forehead, and your dark hair are very beautiful. I wish I had those."

"It hasn't done me any good. Because of my chin and my nose I was known as the scarecrow in elementary school. Things have not changed. Remember, last week I went to a department store in response to a job ad for an office clerk? It was not a sales clerk position but a job in a closed office. The personnel manager told me that the position had already been filled. On the way out, the door still ajar, I noticed that I had left my umbrella in his office. I was just about to reenter when I heard one of the secretaries say: 'Lord, that's all we need around here.' I did not go back in. They still have my umbrella. Yesterday I heard that they finally filled the position with a woman with whom I went to De Anza College. She could be a model in a fashion magazine, but she types only 35 words per minute and does not know shorthand. She never managed to get her AA degree at the community college. Mom, I have been through this too many times."

"Debbie, this hurts us as much as it hurts you. We are all proud of you. Dad and I love you as much as we did when we adopted you 25 years ago. You were not even three years old then. And Ruth likes you a lot. When you were little, we visited two plastic surgeons. Both of them said that surgery would be too risky in your case. You know that already. Just be assured that we love you even more because of that."

"I know you all do, but who else does? At the department store I was not expecting love. I was expecting fairness. Thank God these are not the days of the Salem witch hunt!"

★★★

Deborah stomped out of the house. A sharp wind was blowing. Fall was entering early this year. She saw that Angie and Eric had already joined her dad and Ruth was about to step inside.

"Hi, Ruth. We did not hear your car pull up the driveway. The two sat on the doorsteps and were able to listen in on the conversation between Fred, Angie, and Eric.

"Those are very neat suits your mother bought you," remarked grandpa as he uncapped the honeycombs with his long uncapping knife.

"Why don't you wear a suit?" asked Eric.

"Oh, when you work with bees as often as I do, a little bee sting here or there no longer bothers you. I like to keep them out of my hair, though. That is why I hide my hair under a hankie or a hat."

"Do you get stung often?" asked Angie.

"No, not often because I make slow movements around bees. Jerky movements, especially a hand movement like chasing flies threatens them, and a bee will only sting you when she feels threatened. Wasps, on the other hand, seem to be more aggressive. They are a different breed entirely."

Angie was curious. "If you don't want to threaten the bees, why then do you blow smoke into the beehive when lifting off the top?"

"Good question, Angie. When I blow smoke into the box the bees think that the forest is on fire. Out in the wild the bees move out in a hurry when it burns, but first they fill their honey stomachs with honey. While they are busy doing that they don't bother me, and I can lift out the frames with many bees clinging to them. A bee with her honey stomach full of honey is calm versus a bee that is hungry. That's why, when I want to catch a bee swarm I first sniff it. If I smell honey I am not worried, but if I don't, I assume that they have been hanging in that tree for days and are cranky because they are hungry. Then I wear protective gear. By the way, some popular books tell you that smoke calms bees down. It does not, but it gets them busy and occupied."

"Do drones sting you?"

"No, Eric. Drones have no stingers. They are totally defenseless. They neither defend nor feed themselves. Their sisters, the worker bees, feed them. It is almost 11 o'clock, kids. Let's get this job done."

"Boy, these frames are heavy," said Eric. "That's a lot of honey. If I were a bee I would not take that sitting down if people took my honey."

"They wouldn't either, Eric, if I did not use a smoker. Did you know that during her entire two weeks of foraging the average bee brings home only one teaspoon full of nectar? But multiply that by 10,000 or 20,000 bees foraging, and then multiply that by four generations of bees in one summer. How many teaspoons is that?"

"I can do that," said Angie to Eric's relief. 20,000 times 4 generations comes to 80,000 teaspoons full of nectar."

"Good for you, Angie. And that nectar would turn into almost 80,000 teaspoons of honey if water did not evaporate from the nectar and if the bees did not eat a lot of the nectar and the honey. 5 to 8% of the bees are drones. They do not produce any honey, but they eat."

"How come they are so lazy?" asked Angie.

"Drones have another important function. I'll tell you some other time. We have to get this job done before lunch. We now have to put the frames, five at a time, into the extractor, turn the crank to make it spin at high speed, so that the honey is forced out of the combs. It then runs or drips through this fine screen to filter out all the impurities before it flows into the jars. Here muscle man, show us what you have got," Fred said to Eric.

While Eric was turning the crank with all of his might, Angie looked kind of forlorn. "Are we not mean when we take their honey? What if some big monster with giant arms grabbed into our food pantry and emptied it out?"

"Well Angie, I am glad that you are sensitive, but we always leave them enough honey for the winter. We are not taking anything out of the brood chamber, the big box at the bottom, and between now and October they go on collecting. When bees don't sleep, they always work for the community, never thinking about themselves, always tiring themselves for others. It would be nice if everybody learned a little from them."

"I think Aunt Debbie is like that. She is always doing things for others."

"You are right, Angie. There is a resemblance between her and a honeybee. You ought to become a psychologist."

Eric was moaning. "What is a psychologist? My arms are getting tired."

"Just keep on pushing. You can do it," laughed Angie. "Think of the worker bees."

"Why, the worker bees are all girls. Their brothers don't have to work. You should be turning the crank."

"You can't argue with that," laughed grandpa.

"Psychologist," muttered Eric. "What is a psychologist anyway?"

MÉLISSA

I remember creatures moving up and down outside of the thin walls of wax pressing against my body. I remember how I could sense them but I saw nothing. My surroundings were pitch black. Although nature had endowed me with five eyes, I did not know what light was. Here, however, the floating blue of the sky and the golden rays of the evening sun are lulling me into bliss. Is that what they call animal heaven?

Only five weeks ago my throat was dry and I began to nibble on the walls of my confinement. Ah, the sweet aroma all around me! Whose voices were those outside? "Push, sister, push! My name is Bzz and this is Zmm." My front legs were pulling, my middle legs were scratching, and my hind legs were pushing. I was exhausted but I could suddenly breathe, taking in the sweet aroma and gaining strength.

"Where am I?"

"Come sister, let us show you around in our queendom."

"I am so stiff."

"Patience, sister, patience. You were cooped up in that cell for 18 days."

"My throat is dry."

"Here, take this from me. Put your mouth right up to mine. This is nectar."

Crawling around between hundreds of sisters I could finally feel where the nectar was stored as it slowly turned into honey. Thank God for these antennas, my senses of smell. There was so much to learn. In a few days I was able to feed other babies and my brothers, just as I had been fed, and one day, when I had the privilege to feed the queen, a very rare privilege among so many sisters, I felt very important.

I liked my brothers, the drones. They were furry and roly-poly. The older ones flew out every day looking for young queens to make love to. And when they got a rare chance to do so they never returned. They had to pay with their lives for that rare pleasure. I was so eager to learn.

ERNIE'S VISIT

The Walshes and the Rileys had just sat down for coffee and cake to celebrate Fred's birthday when Ernie Miller, one of the town's wallpaper hangers, showed up. A few weeks earlier he had done the Walsh's master bedroom in return for 10 jars of honey.

"I came to see if, maybe, you had a chance to extract honey. Mom wants to bake baklavas because our Greek friends are coming to visit."

"Got it all done this morning with the help of Eric and Angie here," answered Fred. "I don't know what I would have done without these two. Come, sit down and have a piece of cake and a cup of Debbie's coffee. Ernie sat down across from Ruth, somewhat clumsily for a thirty year old, almost pulling the tablecloth in the process. He seemed tired from hanging wallpaper all day long.

"So, you helped with the extracting," he said to Eric next to him. "Aren't you afraid of bee stings?"

"Nonsense," answered Eric. "A bee sting won't hurt you none. With your finger nail you have to scrape the stinger out of your skin and you won't get much poison."

"How is that?" asked Ernie curiously.

Eric was thinking about an answer he could come up with, but Angie got ahead of him explaining that there are 22 muscles attached to the stinger which keep on pumping venom into you. When a bee stings you, those muscles pull out of the bee's body because at the end of the stinger there are little hooks which get stuck in your skin.

"You two are real pros," answered Ernie. Ruth sat there with her mouth open and Fred smiled with satisfaction.

"Well, we were wearing …" Angie could not finish the statement because Eric kicked her under the table. He did not want outsiders to know they had worn protective suits.

"Macho!" whispered Angie.

Mary changed the topic quickly by asking how Ernie's lady friend Elsa was. Ernie hesitated with his answer. His voice trembled a little: "Oh, it's a long story. We have split up. I believe that she was really after someone else while faking love for me."

That does not seem like Elsa, Deborah thought.

Ruth had been watching Ernie all the time. *He looks quite handsome,* she thought. *Blue eyes, wavy blond hair, strong arms, and not at all arrogant. He needs a new pair of glasses. They don't go with his face. They make him look stupid.*

Too bad she is married, thought Ernie. *I cannot keep my eyes off her reddish-blond French braids, those aquamarine eyes, and those eyelashes. I must not stare at her. What a fool to leave her, taking off with a striptease dancer.* Ernie pretended not to notice her by not gazing at her. Instead, he turned to Deborah with a compliment: "You make excellent coffee. What's your secret?"

"If I told you, it would no longer be a secret, but I'll let you see the bag."

As Deborah limped to the kitchen, Ruth said to Ernie: "Come to the diner some day and I'll tell you the secret."

Deborah came with the coffee bag. "I use Britt coffee from Costa Rica. It's hard to find. The Britt Company picks only ripe berries instead of ripping everything off the bushes and then lets the green ones ripen on trays in the sun. That eliminates a bitter taste from the coffee. And then, to get a smooth taste, you must pour the water on the coffee shortly before it comes to a full boil, before it begins to bubble, unless you use an automatic coffee maker, which I never do. The coffee in offices which boils all day in percolators is awful stuff."

"Especially if it is then served in plastic mugs or Styrofoam cups," added Mary.

"I agree," said Ruth. "Coffee should be served in nice cups. There are more secrets in making good coffee. At the diner, unfortunately, we have to serve the brew in plastic mugs, and their coffee is very diluted. I feel embarrassed serving the brew. The owner wants to save money and thereby only hurts his business. Come to the diner, Ernie, and I'll find you a much nicer cup, and I'll smuggle in a little piece of chocolate for you. Then I'll tell you more about good coffee."

As Deborah took the coffee bag back to the kitchen, she added that a coffee bag, once opened, should be kept in the refrigerator. Fred had a grin on his face and quietly said to Ernie: "No matter what these women tell you, the best coffees are blends of different varieties, but don't drink too much of it. It's bad for your heart." Then he also disappeared to the kitchen.

"What is all this wrapping paper doing here?" asked Ernie.

"Oh my, we forgot to tell you, explained Mary. "Today is Fred's 69th birthday.

Fred came back from the kitchen with five large jars of honey, the equivalent of ten regular jars. "Fresh from the cones," he said to Ernie. "No preservatives." Ernie stood up, raised his empty coffee cup and said: "May the saddest days of your 69th year be no worse than the happiest of the past!"

"That sounds like something my dad used to say way back in Ireland," responded Fred and raised his cup as well, and so did all the others.

Ernie thanked him for the honey and put the jars into a leather bag which he had brought. Ruth followed him to the front porch. "Diner," she whispered to him, and Ernie walked off like in a daze, into the sunny September evening. Ruth noticed two birds piercing the air like black silhouettes against the blue sky.

★★★

"Mom, I think he's falling for her," remarked Deborah.

"Or she for him."

"I am going to hang up the laundry and iron the shirts before seeing Alma for her reading lesson."

"Debbie, the laundry can wait. You need to stop running back and forth the way you do. We should have given you the name Busy Bee when we adopted you. Why, by the way, could Alma's mother not bring her here for the reading lessons, considering that she is paying you peanuts and you don't drive and have a hard time walking?"

"Alma is wheelchair bound and she is afraid of new environments."

Mary raised her finger, shook it and said: "And she will never lose that fear as long as she stays cooped up in her nest."

"Mom, the girl experiences anxiety when they take her some place, and she is not just a paraplegic, she also has a low I.Q."

"Anxiety? Low I.Q.? That is all the more reason why she should be pushed out of her nest and get to take a look beyond that stupid six foot wooden fence they built around their backyard."

"Mom, I feel that I have a role to fulfill in her life. If I don't go she will be worse off." Deborah then took the wash out of the machine and hung it on the laundry line behind the house. Then she ironed the shirts and dashed off limping in a beeline to Alma's place. When Fred entered the house, Mary was standing at the front door cussing: "Her stubbornness makes me want to slap her at times."

"Stubbornness or generosity?" asked Fred.

"Both," answered Mary.

MÉLISSA

When at the age of two weeks I flew out for the first time to gather nectar and pollen, my sisters told me to take it easy. "Who is driving you? Slow down!" I was very ignorant of dangers but I wanted to accomplish things. An orange grove must have been sprayed with a strange smelling and fine mist, maybe to kill the Mediterranean fruit flies. The nectar smelled good and I filled my honey stomach flying from blossom to blossom while pollen stuck to the hair of my legs. On my way home I began to experience excruciating pain, and when I reached my hive, my younger sisters, the guards at the entrance, looked at me funny. One of them was laughing at me. Why?

I did not sleep well and the next morning I decided to stay home, and it wasn't until the following day that I felt fine again, except that there was a burning sensation on the left side of my face. Leaving the hive, where we could see each other in the morning sunlight, I ran into Bzz, an unbelievable occurrence considering the size of our family. I was so happy to see her and wanted to strike up a conversation, but she hushed away saying that she was very busy at that moment and flew into the sunshine. A drone looked at me and said: "uuh," and turned away.

Bewildered I flew out and found a peach tree in bloom. Morning drops were still hanging like crystals from the branches and in one of the water drops I saw my reflection. I almost fainted. The chemicals had deformed one side of my face. It looked disgusting. I was tempted not to fly home but to crawl into a hidden corner and die because I felt that I was no longer fully accepted. Then another feeling grabbed me and told me that there was a purpose in my life and that I had a role to fulfill. After all, I was still one of the fastest fliers, and I said to myself: "Don't be a coward. Never give up!"

Now I miss home, and then again I don't. I am very tired. The golden rays of the evening sun shining through the rose petals and the late September breeze ... Yes, I feel it now: It is like they were carrying me into the unknown. I can't wait to see what the unknown is like. Why are people so fearful of death? These moments are so beautiful. The golden rays, the velvety wind, the sweet aroma of the roses, are all blending into one. ... I feel so lightweight, like floating ... so tranquil ... so ...

MOTHER AND SON

God, what have I done? I am not even divorced yet and might never be. The way he gazes at me leaves little doubt that he likes me. To be honest, I like him too, in spite of his goofy glasses. Nevertheless, he is no match for me. He keeps coming to my house. The diner would be better; it's a public place.

Diner, yes. I must not forget to ask my boss if Debbie could get a job there, part time perhaps. He would, of course, never hire her for the floor. It would have to be a kitchen job, but then, from some of the counter seats you can see the whole kitchen and our two cooks can be embarrassingly insensitive. She cooks much better than they do, but they are the types who would never accept advice from a young woman, and Debbie would interpret their macho attitude as discrimination on other grounds.

I worry about her and have enough problems of my own. Angie and Eric are still confident that Travis will come back with a sack full of money. Eric for sure. To be honest, I am beginning to wish he didn't come back, barring a miraculous conversion. For the sake of the children I would have to play along and pretend to let bygones be bygones. Could I? I don't know. Sometimes I feel like crawling into a corner to die.

★★★

Eric was having his own problems: *I did not do my homework. That's why she is making me pull weeds. Angie is still hiding my slingshot. She and mom always stick together. Schoolbooks are boring. Diagram sentences. "You can learn something and get a good foundation." I am tired of hearing it. Bee keeping is more fun except for turning the crank for half an hour. I bet you they have them with motors. Once I heard grandma say that grandpa is tight with his money. Well, I will have to go on cranking.*

I must see if that bee is still sitting in the rose. No, can't be. It has almost been a week now. I think this one here was the rose tree. … I'll be darned! There she is. I'll poke her a little with a twig. … She is not moving. Of course not, she is dead. Looks so peaceful. I did not know that a dead bee could look so cute. Must be one of grandpa's bees, has three stripes on her abdomen. Why is she staring at me with those three little black eyes in the back of her head? Grandpa calls them ocelli. She is looking at me. I wonder if she can still see me. I am getting out of here. I did not kill her.

WHO?

As on most evenings when the weather was nice, Fred and Mary sat on the front porch watching the sunset while reminiscing. One month after the cab company had laid off Travis, Fred and Mary's house had been broken into. The thief had taken $350, which they had been hiding in a small document file underneath Fred's T-shirts in one of their bedroom dressers. The thief had also taken some of Mary's jewelry, including her two most precious items: a brooch which she had inherited from her mother who had inherited it from her mother, and a diamond ring which Fred had given her on their day of engagement. Both were expensive items. It was strange that none of Deborah's money and jewelry had been taken, even though they lay in the open on top of her dresser.

"The Sheriff's Office never made any progress in the investigation," commented Mary as she looked at her ring fingers.

"No, the only fingerprints they found around the house were ours," answered Fred, "but remember that Ernie stated that on the day of the burglary he saw a teenager run away from the house while carrying a bag. He had no reason to suspect that the boy may actually have been in the house, nor did Ernie know that we were not home that day."

After a while Mary commented: "How stupid of us to leave the back door unlocked; but who would expect this to happen in a little hick town like ours where store owner and street sweeper feel like one family. I am glad that the Sheriff's Office informed the pawnshops within a 20 mile radius describing the brooch and the diamond ring which had the date of our engagement engraved in it: 5-1-1940. Because of the war we were still feeling the tail end of the Great Depression. I always wondered how you managed to pay for such a ring."

"We were in love, Mary. Love makes all things possible."

"We still are, my bee man," answered Mary and put her soft hand on his rough one. As they watched the sunset, Mary repeated: "May 1, 1940."

ERNIE AND CHIP

"Ernie, I am done filling cracks and holes. Let's have our lunch break and then get the wallpaper hung."

"In a minute, Chip. I am almost done mixing the paste."

The two were close friends and often worked together and split the income. This week it was the kitchen of an empty house that was being remodeled. They moved to the desolate family room because two old wicker chairs and a wobbly coffee table had been left there.

"What do you have there, Chip? Peanut butter and jelly sandwiches again?"

"Yep, my seven year old daughter made them for me."

"You should use jam instead of jelly. Jelly is all sugar."

"What do you have?"

"Marinated artichokes, garlic bread and horse beans in garlic. You should try it. It is good for your blood circulation. I eat it all the time."

"Garlic? Man, how often have you kissed her?"

"Kissed whom?"

"Whom? Whom? Ruth, of course."

"I don't have the guts. Haven't found the right moment."

"Ernie, you have to get rid of your shyness. You must strike while the iron is hot."

"I can't help it. I did see her last Saturday at the diner."

"Well, that's progress. Finally!"

"I just happened to pass by there on the way home from a painting job at the Wynberries'. It happened to be the lunch hour."

"And? Did you tell her how pretty she looks in her waitress' uniform? Women like to hear things like that."

"She was very busy. They seemed to be understaffed that day. In a way I did not mind. Haven't worked up the courage to tell her."

"There we go again. Your damn shyness! Women don't like shy men. They want you to appear strong and a little bold."

"I don't know. It would not be proper at this time. She is still married. On the other hand, everything about her mesmerizes me, her French braids, her forehead, her eyes, the way she walks, you name it, … but she is still married. It was dumb of me to stop there in the first place. I hadn't shaven in two days and my hands and pants still had paint spots on them."

"Well Ernie, I might as well tell you now: Your glasses are as ill fitting as your pants. You walk around like a tramp."

"I felt like a tramp when she could free herself for a few minutes and sit with me. She said that two waitresses had called in sick that morning. I reminded her that she wanted to tell me her secrets about brewing good coffee when her boss at the cash register called: 'Mrs. Riley, table #8 needs you.' The hostess had seated a family of five at the table. The kids behaved like a pack of wild dogs, and the parents took 10 minutes to make up their minds and then changed the order twice."

"How did Ruth take that?"

"I could not get over her calmness and politeness. I bet you that she is the one who keeps the customers coming to the diner because her boss is an s. o. b. I had expected her to stomp into the kitchen with the order, but she walked as gracefully, almost weightlessly, as always. Simply intoxicating."

"Wow, you were smitten! What the hell are you waiting for? Tell her how you feel. It might speed up the divorce."

"She came back to sit with me again and I told her that I had come to hear about Deborah's secrets of brewing coffee, but that was a lie. I had come to see her and I think that she read my mind."

"Women can psych you out in a few minutes," interrupted Chip.

"I asked her if she had heard from Travis and she told me that there had not been a sign from him for four weeks, but that her in-laws in Los Angeles kept her informed. He had told them that he was doing it all for his family. He also told them that, in order to save money, he and Isabel are sharing a one-bedroom apartment but that he sleeps on the sofa while she has the bedroom. They believe that no more than Ruth and I do, but they do believe that he may be doing it all for his family.

Ruth had tears in her eyes as she related all of that to me. What makes a man leave such a beautiful wife?"

"Well, he is gone. He will never be back. Now is the time to throw the lasso," said Chip as he lit a cigarette.

"How could I? Travis may well be back some day and shed crocodile tears. I really felt like hugging her when she had another break and we stepped outside for a few minutes, but all we talked about was coffee. Sometimes she slips small pieces of chocolate into the coffee pot. It works miracles she told me with a mischievous smile."

"Coffee is all you talked about when you were outside? I give up. Let's hang the wallpaper now before I start crying." Chip drew the last smoke out of his cigarette.

The next day Chip went to the Walshes to reattach the wallpaper in a few areas of the master bedroom because Ernie had inadvertently used cheap and defective paste. Deborah sat on her mother's bed watching Chip while they talked about Ernie.

"I cannot believe it," said Chip.

"Believe what?"

"How can a man be so shy? This is the third time he lets a fish slip out of his net."

"What are you talking about?"

"I am talking about Ernie and your sister."

"I would not exactly call her a fish in his net."

"But there were others," Chip explained. The first time it was Aiicia Hernández. She mesmerized him with her long and shiny black ponytail, her beautiful eyebrows and her dimples. He could not sleep anymore. She was a postal clerk manning a window at the post office in East Palo Alto. He must have driven to that post office twice a week to buy some stamps or have a letter weighed, and each time he managed to slip into some spot in the waiting line so as to end up at her window. What he did not know was that some bully, a member of a drug gang, also had an eye on Alicia. She did not have a car and took the bus to work. One day Ernie decided to offer Alicia a ride home which she gladly accepted. To get to know her better he decided to treat her to a drink at a bar near her apartment. Had he known that it was such a dark and spooky place, he would have chosen a better lit bar. They were sipping Martinis and Ernie was holding Alicia's hand when a husky guy in a leather motorcycle jacket approached the table and said to Ernie: 'Hey punk, you are at my table.'

'Your table? What are you talking about?' Ernie let Alicia's hand go.

'You keep your hands off my broad,' warned the drug dealer, and because Ernie would not move, the gangster knocked Ernie's Martini glass off the table, pulled him by his necktie from the chair and said: 'You show your funny face here again and your nose will be a pancake.'

"I never heard of that story before. It's interesting. Go on."

"That same evening Ernie talked to one of his uncles about it, a retired Rabbi."

"I did not know that Ernie was Jewish."

"He is not, the Millers are Catholic, but that uncle is on the mother's side. They are Jewish and attend the synagogue. From what he told me, the conversation went something like this:

'What am I going to do? I know she loves me.'

'How do you know that she loves you?'

'I can tell by the way she looks at me.'

'Talk to her, but not in a bar. Have you ever told her that you love her?'

"Not yet. Haven't worked up the courage."

"Do it and see how she reacts. Be a little daring, but do not, and I say it again, do not mess with him and stay away from that bar. He who lives by the sword, dies by the sword. The proverb scared Ernie and he never went back to that post office to have his letters weighed.

She was a very fine woman and he should have rescued her from that motor cycle punk."

"Poor Ernie! He needs a strong woman," commented Deborah. All the while she felt a little guilty listening to all of this because she was almost certain that the information Ernie had given Chip was meant to be confidential, but then curiosity drowned out her conscience.

"One year later, a woman by the name of Elsa asked Ernie if he could do a wall papering job for her in the bedroom of her condo. She was a redhead with blue eyes and baby soft skin."

"I know her," interrupted Deborah, "but go on."

"They agreed on the terms, and in order to get the job done quickly, she helped him with the hanging of the paper. He was quite impressed by her skills and thought that she could have done the job by herself. As she was standing on the ladder wearing a mini skirt, he almost lost his sanity. Lying awake in bed at night he began to fantasize how the two could be in business together, double his income, and sleep wrapped up in each other's arms."

"Well, what ended it?" Deborah was anxious to hear. "Poor Ernie! He sees a devil behind every wall. One day he noticed that there was someone else after her who actually forced a kiss on her. Ernie got the impression that she did not mind. When Ernie took Elsa out to dinner a few days later, he also got the impression that she was not as talkative as she had been at other occasions, and because she had ordered a rather expensive dish, he immediately concluded that she was taking advantage of him."

"I happen to know her from high school," Deborah explained. She is the type who plays hard to catch."

Chip shook his head and said: "Poor Ernie. He does not understand women. And now he is letting another fish get loose. All they talked about was coffee."

"I don't know what coffee has to do with this."

"He met your sister Ruth at a restaurant the other day. And all they talked about was coffee."

"How would you know that?"

"He told me."

"Chip, it would be wise if all of this would remain confidential, because he opens up to you as a friend, and he trusts you with that."

"I am afraid you may be right, but I think that your sister ought to know that he loves her, but all they talked about was coffee."

HAPPY INTERLUDE

Fred's pickup truck pulled into the driveway. He had been away for three days attending a convention of the Beekeepers Association. He was hardly out of the car when Mary ran into the garage yelling: "Fred, come inside. Hurry up!" Fred paid little attention to it knowing how hyper Mary could get over nothing.

"Fred, Ruth called a few minutes ago. Come inside and listen to what I have to tell you."

"What, my dear?"

"She said that she won in the state lottery, and she won big."

"How many drinks did you have while I was gone? Are you forgetting that today is the first of April?"

"No, Fred. Ruth would not joke about something like that."

"How much did she win?"

"$10,200. First I thought that it was one of her sarcastic jokes. You never think that it could happen to someone in your own family. It's always people far away and usually to rich people."

"$10,200," repeated Fred. "Are you sure?"

"That's what she said."

"Let's drink to that!" shouted Fred, turning hyper himself. He went to the basement to get a bottle of Hearty Burgundy. At that moment

Ernie came rushing into the house, threw the local newspaper on the kitchen table and said: "The whole town will know about it before the day is up. I cannot stay because I am in the middle of a paint job. See you soon. Bye."

When Fred came up with the bottle, Mary showed him the paper. "See, it's right here on the first page."

WHEEL OF FORTUNE STOPS AT MOUNTAIN VIEW

A local resident, Mrs. Ruth Riley, won this week's lottery. The total amount of $30,600 will be split evenly between three contestants granting each player $10,200. The other winners are a mailman in Sacramento and a bus driver in Palo Alto.

"Fred, can they publicize that without Ruth's permission?"

"I don't know what the law says about that. If there is anyone who needs the dough now, it's Ruth. Nevertheless, knowing Ruth, she is going to split it with Debbie."

"How much might they deduct for taxes?"

"Between Federal and State, anywhere between 2,000 and 3,000, but 8,000 is still a nice sum. Cheers to our daughter and the lottery!"

After a while, Mary sounded annoyed saying: "I wish they had not published that. Ruth is now going to be pestered with letters and phone calls from fundraising organizations."

Fred was stuffing his pipe and looked at the blurb in the paper again oblivious to what Mary was saying.

———— DEBORAH AND MRS. CRAWFISH ————

"What can I do for you, Miss Walsh?"

She looks like a commanding military officer. All she needs are epaulets with stars on her navy-type jacket. She must run this public library with an iron hand. I better be brief and to the point.

"Mrs. Crawfish, I appreciate it very much that you agreed to see me at such short notice."

"Well, at this library we are here for the community. What's on your mind?"

"Mrs. Crawfish, I have been giving private lessons in reading and writing to illiterate adults, often free of charge. It is something I like to do."

"You wouldn't be a school teacher?"

"No, but I think that I am good at it, and I have often regretted the fact that I did not attend a teachers college. I brought copies of my high school and community college transcripts showing that I have close to a 4.0 GPA."

Mrs. Crawfish studied the college transcript. "Very impressive, indeed. There is something strange about your name: Deborah Teresa Walsh. Teresa has an h missing."

"Well, when I was baptized, that was on October 15, the feast day of the sixteenth century saint, Teresa of Avila. The priest thought that I should have a saint's name. They chose Teresa as it was spelled in Spanish. My parents must have liked the name."

"What do you mean by *must have liked the name*? Did you never ask them?"

"My parents died when I was a toddler. It seems that none of my uncles and aunts wanted me. I was then shipped from foster home to foster home until I was adopted a year later. Now here is why I need to talk to you. I have been teaching most of those people in their homes because I don't have a classroom. Our house is not suited for teaching classes. I don't drive and taking public transportation to different homes is very time consuming. Would it perhaps be possible to have them come here for tutoring sessions? Might there be a small room available for small groups, once or twice a week?" Deborah sounded anxious.

"Groups? How many students do you have?"

"At this time only three whom I meet in three different places. If we had one convenient location and if we advertised the classes, there could easily be several groups of five students each."

"Why do you want it to grow? Don't you have anything else to do?"

"Mrs. Crawfish, you have no idea how exciting and rewarding it is when you see that proud feeling of accomplishment on their faces when they write their names, addresses, and birthdates for the first time. Some of them are Mexican immigrants and have a double problem, but I know enough Spanish to explain English to them as well."

Mrs. Crawfish gave Deborah a skeptical look. "How old are you?"

"Almost 26."

"Almost 26 and not certified?"

"These people need help, Mrs. Crawfish. No one else around here is doing it."

Deborah's concern sounded genuine to Mrs. Crawfish and she responded with a rare degree of feeling.

"Well, we happen to have two small rooms available on certain days. That ought to do as long as the program does not grow by leaps and bounds, which I doubt it will." Mrs. Crawfish studied Deborah with piercing eyes. "If you do as good a job as you think you will, it might actually look good for this public library. What about fees? As head of the library I have to meet large overhead expenses."

Deborah had been afraid of that question. She had been unrealistically hoping that it would not come up. "I charge them moderate amounts, all depending on their income. Sometimes I get paid with a dinner invitation."

"Now wait a minute, young lady. We cannot run a library on dinner invitations. We have to charge you a room fee, regardless of the number of students."

"How much would that be?"

"How would $10.00 per hour per room strike you?"

Deborah's enthusiasm seemed shaken, but soon she regained her self-confidence and she calculated: "Having three students that would come to $3.30 per class per student. I could easily get a fourth student lowering the fee to $2.50. Even Mrs. Alvarado, who holds a minimum wage job, has a little boy and an ailing mother to support, might be able to pay that."

"And what about your fee? You also need to make a living."

"I only charge if the student can pay."

"Not a good policy. Not a good policy at all. People will take advantage of you claiming poverty. Also, when services are free, people tend to take them for granted."

"I trust that God will provide."

"You trust ... well, then have it your way."

"In other words, we can use the library?"

"You may, but there better be no unpleasant surprises like taco wrappings on the table. There is to be no eating, drinking or smoking in the library. Water is okay."

"Mrs. Crawfish, I'll see to it that the rooms are left as clean as we find them."

"Alright then, let's call it the ABC program. You may start this Saturday if you wish. Each time you will have to ask for the key at the circulation desk."

"Thank you, Mrs. Crawfish. You have been most kind and understanding."

As Deborah went out the door, one of the other librarians heard Mrs. Crawfish mumbling to herself: "It's going to be a flop. With that face she is not going to have much of a following, but I wish her luck."

THE PLEA

Deborah sat down for the third time to write Travis a letter. On the floor lay several crumpled up sheets from earlier attempts.

My Dear Brother-in-law,

It has been almost three months now that you left Ruth and the children. Several times I started to write to you but never could find the right words. Three times I tore up the letter half way through because my emotions always got the better of me. Ruth and my parents know nothing about this letter.

There are situations when separation or divorce is unavoidable. That, however, was not the case in your marriage. Ruth loved you and you loved her and the children. Why then did you leave? Why has Ruth received only a few lines from you, greetings bare of any meaningful content. I feel that I can be very open with you because you and I have always gotten along so well. You cannot blame Ruth or me for getting the impression that Isabel's good looks and skills as a dancer are the key. She may well be a topnotch dancer, but her beauty is on the surface, it seems, if the rumors about her reputation are true. Was it Isabel or was it your unemployment or both that drove you to the bottle? Travis, this is strictly between you and me: If the rumors are true, she is poison for you. Given the possibility that they are not true, I want to keep this remark confidential.

I remember how enthusiastically you answered the priest on your wedding day with "I do," when asked whether you would honor and love Ruth, for better and for worse, in sickness and in health, for as long as you live.

I beg you to come back to the family without Isabel. If you do, you will earn no criticism from me. On the contrary, if you do come back I will hold you in the highest esteem because such a step shows courage. I know that you have many fine qualities. Angie and Eric miss you, and Eric needs a father as a role model. If you love your children, you will dump the wetback and come home. A willing heart sees nothing as impossible. If you answer me, I promise you, that whatever you write, will be kept in strict confidence between you and me.

With love and concern,
Deborah

N.B. I got carried away using a derogatory title for Isabel. I should not have done that because she did not swim the Rio Grande. You once told me that she is half Cuban, on her mother's side and that she lived in New Orleans before coming to California. I am sorry, but keep in mind that more than once she has referred to me as "*that hunchback.*" By the way, I got your mailing address from your dad.

The day after the letter had arrived, Isabel's curiosity got the upper hand. *I wonder why Travis shut the dresser drawer so quickly when I came home unexpectedly last night. He won't be here for another hour. Let's see. T-shirts, underwear, socks, hankies. I wish he would use Kleenex instead of these new handkerchiefs when his fingers are messy. He has got fruit stains on them, and this one he must have used when working on his Pontiac... Men! ... Ah, here, there is an envelope under his socks. A letter. I'll be darned! It's a letter from Deborah Walsh.*

Isabel's face turned red as she read. Then she yelled out: "That holier than thou bastard! So, I am poison for Travis. I come with a bad reputation. I am the cause for his drinking. Oh, I hate that hunchback!" I don't think that Travis should grace her with a response, but if he does, he should tell her to go to hell. What's between Travis and Ruth and between Travis and me is none of that scarecrow's business. I will remember the letter well.

HOMECOMING

Ruth was sure she had a vision when, one day, she saw Travis pulling up on the driveway in his old Pontiac. She noticed a Nevada license plate. He rang the doorbell. She had to dry her hands first because she was in the midst of cleaning the kitchen.

For a while they faced each other without saying a word until Travis blared out: "Hey Ruth. Long time no see."

"Long time no see," she answered almost inaudibly.

"Aren't you going to invite me in?"

Ruth was still in a trance. "Of course. Come in. The floor is wet. I am cleaning house. What brings you back all the way from Vegas? Have you two broken up? Let's sit in the living room. The floor in the kitchen is still wet."

"We have not broken up because there is nothing to break up. There is nothing intimate between us." There was silence for a while until Travis said: You don't believe me, do you?"

"How stupid do you think I am?"

"No, Ruth, you are still my wife. I am not at all happy about you wanting a divorce. Why a divorce? I have great plans for the children and us. I am going to convert an old pawnshop into a nightclub in a hot tourist spot in Vegas and I need Isabel as a dancer. That's why I asked her to come with me."

"In other words, you had it all planned by the time you left but you never told me anything about it. You deserted me, and how come you hardly ever wrote to me and never called? I had to get your address from your parents."

"I wanted to surprise you when it was all done, and I was too busy negotiating with the contractors. Believe me, I was doing it all for us."

"Why didn't you explain that from the beginning instead of sneaking out with that striptease dancer?"

"I did not sneak out with her. I need her for our new business."

"But you two have been living together for the last six months in a one-bedroom apartment."

"That was just to save money. How did you know that?"

"Let's just say that I found out. And you cannot tell me that there are no dancers available in Las Vegas of all places. Did it ever occur to you that I might want to have a say about living in Las Vegas and raising our children in that sin city? Travis, after 14 years of marriage I can sense whether you are lying or telling the truth. You are the most cunning liar on this planet."

Ruth could not hide her anger and went to the kitchen. Travis followed her and said in a sarcastic tone: "And what about you and that wallpaper hanger?"

"What do you expect? You give almost no sign of life for six months, barring a few short sentences telling me that you are too busy to write much, you don't tell me what you are up to, you live with another woman in a small one-bedroom apartment, and you expect me to hold on to you? 'I am doing it all for us.' Insulting. And for your information: Ernie and I have never slept together, nor have we ever kissed."

"Ruth, my dear, calm down. Anger has gotten the best of you. I admit, I have gone about it in a dumb way, but the truth is that I meant well. If I can get the place ready before New Year's, we can reap in $1,000 in one evening. Wouldn't you prefer to live in a mansion instead of this matchbox of ours? We could eventually have a house with two fireplaces and maid service. I could have the club ready soon but I desperately need $4,000. That is less than half of what your lottery ticket netted you."

"So that's why you came to see me. Where did you get that information?"

"Let's just say I found out."

Ruth turned red in her face. "Whose idea was it to come here for money, yours or Isabel's?" There followed a minute of painful silence until Ruth had calmed down a little, looked her husband in the eye and said: "What I won in the lottery is far less than what our family would have received over the past six months had you not driven your cab under the influence of booze, and had you not left us but accepted another job even if you felt that it was below your majesty's dignity. I work overtime at the diner to make ends meet and you want to take $4,000 from the children and me?"

"But Ruth, it would all come back to the family. I am doing it for us."

"For your information," answered Ruth, "Las Vegas is one of the last places on his planet where I would want to live and raise our children."

At that Travis turned around, accidentally knocked over a vase with roses, and stomped out of the house. He came back just to say: "Let's talk again when you are in a better mood."

★★★

In their motel room, the following day, Isabel was leafing through the local newspaper. "Travis, did you see today's paper? On the front page of the local news it says: ABC PROGRAM AT THE PUBLIC LIBRARY IS GROWING. They teach grownups reading and writing. Half of them are Mexican immigrants. They must be new wetbacks."

"How would you know that?"

"If they weren't they would know how to read."

"Gibberish, Isabel. I remember you telling me that one of your Cuban grandfathers came to this country as a stowaway on a ship to New Orleans and that he was hired by the New Orleans Symphony to play the violin."

"Yes, but he was of British origin. He was a Macintosh, and he had studied Music in college. After coming to Havana he played with the Havana Symphony. My mother was Cuban, María Sánchez, but I go by Macintosh."

"Isabel, you are a snob and a racist."

As Isabel was tying her shiny long and fiery hair in a bun, Travis again felt that attraction for her. Isabel radiated a charm which drew him to her like a powerful magnet in spite of the many dust and dirt particles between them. He would have hugged and kissed her had she not been uttering words like: "Hm, racist. Great idea."

"What are you saying?"

"They have three instructors, and guess who is in charge of the program."

"Who? … Stop that condescending smile and tell me who."

"That young misfit, your sister-in-law."

"Impossible. She has no teacher training."

"Here, read for yourself."

"I'll be damned. Well, she does have a high IQ. In high school and in community college she got almost straight A's. There is a difference between you and her. While both of you are very gifted, she is a book worm and you are allergic to books."

"Travis, she hates me. A year ago, when we got into an argument, she thought that I was Mexican and she called me a wetback. Remember?"

"She only called you that because you had hurt her feelings by calling her a hunchback."

"She despises me. Why?"

"Not because she thought that you were Mexican but for the same reason Ruth despises both of us. ... Tell you the truth, I am no longer sure that I should blame them for that."

Isabel did not respond to that statement but said: "She probably doesn't give a damn about the wetbacks. The program gives her a chance to show the world that she has made it in life and also to pat her bank account."

"No, my dear, you got that wrong. It says here that the three teachers are providing the service free of charge. The students are only charged the room rent. It also says that the program is well received by the adult learners. They are not all immigrants either. One is already in his seventies."

"But the scarecrow has no teacher training. You said it yourself."

"Did you have dancer training before you started hopping around and swinging your fanny on the platform of the Starlight? Admit it: You were hired for your looks."

"She was born 'una bastarda,' from what I heard."

"She was not. Her parents died when she was very little, and if she had been 'una bastarda,' would that have been her fault? The derogatory descriptions you use for her bother me a lot. I wish you would cut that out. Deborah cannot help her fate."

"She is mean."

"She happens to have a very pleasant personality and a winning smile, far from that of a scarecrow."

"How come you are always protecting her?"

"She and I have always been on good terms. I don't want to spoil that. Why don't you put yourself into her shoes for a while? What do you have against the ABC program?"

"She wrote to you calling me 'poison.' She wrote that I had a bad reputation and that I was responsible for your drinking. She is a jealous bitch."

"I see you have been snooping in my drawers."

"I only wanted to see if your socks needed mending and there was that letter. She used the term wetback again, just because I speak Spanish.

"When has the world ever seen you mending socks? And let me explain to you once more: Her use of that term was an emotional reaction to you referring to her as 'that hunchback'. Outbursts like that are not to be taken seriously."

"Well, she is a hunchback while I am no wetback. Her students will find out from whom they are taking instruction."

"No. Please don't. She does not hate you. That's all in your head. You are the jealous one, not she. She has not had it easy. Don't destroy the little niche she has built for herself, and do not forget that I will never get my share of the money if you malign her and Ruth finds out. I thought my getting half of the money was so important to you. I am at the verge of dropping the claim for the sake of the children. As badly as I need it to establish the new club, I would not have asked for it, had I not felt that I was going to lose you by not trying to get it. A crack is developing in our relationship."

"You would get the money if you weren't such a wimp. I thought that legally you two owned everything in common like in a good marriage. So then make your legal claim."

"Did you call me a wimp? A person who cannot muster any will power when she sees a pack of cigarettes or a bottle of rum is a wimp."

"Damn you!"

MÉLISSA

I remember early on, when I was still young, that we were getting rather crowded in our beehive. Too many bees. It was getting unbearably hot inside our domain, and that in the middle of July. It could have turned into a bitter struggle with all of us becoming irritated, but no, we felt for each other. We did the best we could to console one another. Those who were already a week old put their wings into overdrive to make the air circulate. Nevertheless, tension was high until the queen and the older bees decided that it was time for "queendom" to split up. She got ready to move out and thousands of bees began to move around nervously, filled themselves with honey, and followed her into uncertainty. People call that swarming. I decided to stay with my younger siblings. The next day, earlier than I was allowed to, I flew out on my own and spotted the escapees as they were hanging like a brown and pointed sack from a tree branch, all clinging to each other like moving coffee beans. Scouts were flying in all directions looking for possible nesting places.

In anticipation of the queen leaving, my older sisters had already begun to raise two new queens. That was no easy job. The two larvae, chosen to become queens, needed constant attention. For five and one half days they were fed some disgusting stuff called royal jell. It was a mixture of pollen, nectar, body secretions and saliva. That made the larvae grow into double sized grubs and then double sized pupae. Their cells had to be enlarged to look like peanut shells, large enough for the pupae to grow into full size queens. And then the most wonderful thing happened: 16 days after the eggs had been laid, 8 days after the peanut shells had been sealed, both queens emerged at the same time, one more beautiful than the other. We were ready for some action, for a duel between these two queens because only one queen governs a bee colony. But no, they seemed to respect and tolerate each other and kept a safe distance from each other, until one of them decided to move out as well, again with thousands of bees, but fewer than were in the first group. People call that an after-swarm. The next day I could not wait to sneak out to see where this after-swarm would form a tongue of moving coffee beans, but I never found them. I missed them a lot, but now we had plenty of space in which to live and grow, and nobody had gotten hurt.

ISABEL'S CURSE

"Debbie, I read in the paper that your ABC program is growing. What is the matter? Have you been crying?" Ruth leaned back studying Deborah's teary eyes.

"If you look at numbers, yes, the program is flourishing. My group has grown from three to six adults. But I don't know why she would do a thing like that. Isabel, that dancer, was at the library, not to read -- God forbid – but to spread rumors. When I arrived she pretended not to see me and she quickly left."

"What kind of rumors?"

"The six students I had today, four of whom are Mexican immigrants, looked at me with some sort of suspicion as I entered the seminar room. After class I cornered José and asked him what went wrong. He told me that some woman who claimed to know me well had told Lía and Yolanda in Spanish, as they were waiting before class, that I had referred to Mexicans as 'those dumb wetbacks.' Never in my life did I do that. Only once did I give Isabel the title 'wetback,' not 'dumb wetback,' because she kept referring to me as 'that hunchback.' That was just a spontaneous outburst in a moment of anger."

After some silence Ruth said: "I am going to talk to Travis. It's time for him to find out with whom he is in love."

"The next item is as stupid a thing as you will ever hear, so stupid that I don't know whether I should laugh it off or cry. We were spelling the word *invalid* and someone asked me what it meant. I explained with an example as I always do: If a person got hit by a car and is now in a wheelchair, that person is an *invalid*. Everybody understood, no problem. But before leaving the library, Giang Nguyen was handed a note by a library staff member telling him that his driving permit which he had left at the circulation desk when applying for a library card had become *invalid*, and that he should drop by the circulation desk on his way out to pick it up.

"He is not the brightest, and ill tempered as he sometimes is, he argued with the desk clerk saying: 'How can a driving permit be *an invalid*?' "When she pointed at the expiration date and explained to him what the word meant, he apparently became convinced that I had misled the class by telling a lie. 'José,' I said, 'if I tell you that *pelota* means ball, and then you find out that the word ball has two other meanings, does that make me a liar?'

'Of course not, I am not stupid like Giang, but he believes it,' answered José. 'He had been told that the woman had called you a racist. I know that it is hogwash, but some people believe in hogwash.' ... Ruth, I am going with you to confront her in the presence of Travis."

"Let's be very careful, Debbie. That type can do more harm to you than she has already done."

During the conversation dark clouds had begun to move in from the Pacific darkening the sky. "Debbie, let me take you home. I see you have no umbrella with you. You'll get wet." As they were driving, Ruth noticed that Deborah had tears rolling down her cheeks, which was unusual for Deborah. Ruth steered the car with her left hand and put her right hand on Deborah's in Deborah's lap.

MRS. CRAWFISH AND STAFF

For the weekly conference with the staff, Mrs. Crawfish walked into the conference room looking frightfully stern. Mike Wilkins, the man in charge of audiovisual equipment, who in college had taken a course on Greek Mythology, was heard whispering: "Amazons still exist."

"Ladies and Gentlemen, today's meeting will be brief. I am certain that you have become aware of a delicate situation here at the library. I have hesitated for several days to come out with this, but to break it to you bluntly: Miss Walsh has become an embarrassment for us. I assume that you know to what I am referring. We cannot afford this kind of publicity, and I regret that we have to tell her to leave. In fact, I think that we should phase out the entire ABC program and use that as a justification to terminate her services. I want to avoid legal challenges."

The conference room fell silent. Only the sound of a distant train could be heard. With apparent shyness, one of the senior librarians ended the impasse by asking, almost inaudibly, as if being afraid of her: "Mrs. Crawfish, are you sure that publicity, which is based on nothing but rumors, is your motive? After all, your dislike for Miss Walsh has been no secret."

Mrs. Crawfish turned red in the face. Her underlings around the conference table expected the Amazon to explode, but giving Mrs. Crawfish no chance to formulate an answer, Juanita González objected with more gusto: "We all know that the allegations are false or, at best, exaggerations."

"She stands accused of telling lies and discriminating against certain minorities like yours, Mrs. González."

"Accused, but not convicted," answered Mike Wilkins.

"Mr. Wilkins, the public will believe the accusations when they hit the newspaper," Mrs. Crawfish answered less forcefully.

"If you kill her program, Mrs. Crawfish, you shatter the only great accomplishment of a very capable but equally vulnerable young woman who has traveled a rough road uphill." Mr. Wilkins sounded compassionate as he said that, which surprised the others as he was known for his occasional outbursts.

Puzzled and annoyed, Mrs. Crawfish snapped back: "Teaching the ABC's is not the job of the public library. People have questioned me on that, and now I think that it was a mistake to give it the go-ahead. It is the job of community colleges and adult education programs with certified instructors. Illiterates are free to check out our first grade readers."

"I took English at the community college and I know that they have no literacy program," replied Juanita.

"But Miss Walsh has no teacher training and we have to uphold standards at our library," Mrs. Crawfish explained.

Mike Wilkins interjected: "Miss Walsh has no teacher training, true, but that was known when you approved the program. She does have an Associate of Arts degree and she has been doing a darn good job."

"… and for free," added someone else. "And the public knows that it is not a program for academic credit. It only helps illiterates to compete in a tough world."

"And the next person will come and want to teach cake decorating or dog grooming for no credit so that people can compete in a tough world," shouted Mrs. Crawfish.

"Those are lame comparisons," remarked Mike.

Mrs. Crawfish straightened up radiating her usual aura of authority. "Alright then. I thank you for your input because I believe in democracy where everyone's voice should be heard. I'll submit the case to the city council and let them decide. Personally, I still think that the program should at least be phased out by not admitting any new students for lack of qualified personnel and because of adverse publicity. There is no need for you to take out time from your busy schedules here to attend the council meeting." Having said that, Mrs. Crawfish slammed the conference folder closed and stated: "For the time being the ABC program is on hold pending a final decision by the city council."

The staff members were dumbfounded, and after she left, Mike Wilson said: "I pity her husband."

★★★

The library staff always treated each employee whose birthday it was to a little reception during the lunch hour. Today's reception was in honor of Juanita González who had reached the golden age of 50. That called for a prolonged lunch hour. The table in the lunch room had been set with colorful paper plates, cups and napkins in red, green and white, the colors of the Mexican flag. Juanita, although legally in the U.S. with a valid work permit, was still a Mexican citizen and she had remained proud of her home country. The bulletin board had been decorated with a photo collage, which Juanita's husband had secretly loaned to the library staff. They showed Juanita at the age of four on a swing set enjoying life to the fullest. Then you could see her riding a mule at the age of 12 in the arid hills of Chihuahua. Staff members commented on how slim and petite she had been with big eyes and French braids. There was also the picture of her little daughter who on her first birthday was digging her hands into the birthday cake with cake and icing all over her face. The last photo showed Juanita with Deborah, the ABC instructor. The two had become friends and Juanita had invited her to the party but Deborah chose not to accept because she feared that her presence would spoil the event, assuming that Mrs. Crawfish would also be there.

Right before the ceremonial cutting of the cake, Mrs. Crawfish entered and said: "I did not want to miss the opportunity to wish Mrs. González all the best for the next 50 years. Congratulations, Juanita. It is fair to say that the entire library staff is happy to have you on board."

That caught Juanita by surprise because many times the two had not seen eye to eye on a variety of issues. Mrs. Crawfish had also signed the birthday card. "I have good news for you," she said, when the staff was enjoying a piece of the rich cake.

"This morning I received word from the city council that the ABC program will not be eliminated, that it is only on hold until a replacement for Miss Walsh can be found."

There was dead silence in the room until Mike Wilson broke the impasse by offering Mrs. Crawfish a piece of the high cholesterol cake.

"No thanks," Mrs. Crawfish said, "I need to watch my figure. A cup of tea would do me just fine. I wish to run this library for 25 more years, God permitting."

Apparently, she did not hear that someone in the back mumbled: "God, save us!"

HIDING

"That's the Sunset Lodge," said Ruth.

"What a dump!" answered Deborah.

"Debbie, control yourself when we confront the dancer. You are apt to make things worse."

"How can they get worse than they already are?"

The barefoot and unshaven grouch behind the reception desk was hesitant to give out any information. "For legal reasons," he said. Ruth had to identify herself first as Mrs. Riley and produced a family photo on which Travis could clearly be identified. "Room 24," said the clerk."

Ruth knocked on the door of room 24.

"Who is it?" Travis yelled from the inside.

"It's Ruth."

"Wait a second. I have to put on a shirt."

After one minute Travis opened the door and said: "How nice of you two to stop by! I only wish you had told me. We could have met at a nicer place than this barn. We are thinking of moving into a boarding house where one pays by the month rather than by the day."

"This barn will do just fine," remarked Deborah. "We were hoping to find Isabel."

"She went to the club."

"I guess that's where she belongs." Deborah sounded sarcastic and Travis could not hide a feeling of discomfort.

"Let me turn off the TV set," he said and ran to the bathroom like a chicken without a head, came right back and fumbled with the TV controls. Apparently he had been looking for the remote control in the bathroom but could not find it.

"We were hoping to find Isabel," Deborah said once more.

"Why?"

"Don't you know what she has done to me?"

"I don't know what you are talking about."

"You mean to tell me that you don't know about the rumors she spread about me at the library?"

"No, what kind of rumors?"

"She told my students that I was a racist and that I disliked Mexicans, and that I didn't give a damn about them, that I only taught for the recognition and the money. The word has spread and is still circulating."

"No. Why would she do a thing like that? That does not sound like Isabel at all. There must be a misunderstanding. Let me ask her tonight."

"It's too late now," Ruth interrupted. "The damage has been done. They had a meeting of the library staff and Debbie has been told to leave. Who knows if after this she will ever get hired any place?"?"

"Now wait a little. I do not believe that Isabel did that. And furthermore: Debbie, with your high I.Q. you will get hired at some other place."

"You know better than that," yelled Ruth. Her voice trembled. If you really believe that Isabel is innocent, you do not know the woman you ran off with. You must either be awfully stupid or madly in love."

"Talking about stupid! If you had loaned me the $4,000, we would have been out of here the next day and I would be building our future."

"Last time we talked it did not sound like a loan. I tell you what. You get rid of your striptease dancer, get rid of her for good, and I'll give you what you perceive to be your share. That's a promise."

"You really hate her, don't you? I have told you before and I say it again: There is nothing intimate between us." Travis said it rather quietly and sounded like a broken record as he continued: "I only need her to build up and run the business in Vegas. After that she and I can split. You ought to be grateful that I am doing that."

That aggravated Ruth. "Travis, you seem to ignore completely the objections which I voiced during your surprise visit two weeks ago -- my objections to living in Las Vegas. You must think that I am both blind and stupid. Come, Debbie. Let's go and find her at the Starlight." No sooner had they left and were out of sight when Travis yelled toward the bathroom: "You can come out now. They are gone." Isabel was mad. "You were a wimp again," she said, to which Travis answered: "Cry if it makes you feel better."

ANIMAL HEAVEN?

"Grandpa, I wish we had a porch like this. I would do all of my homework and write all of my letters on it."

"I love it, too. I would not want to do without it. Many an evening we sit here watching the sunset. The sky and the clouds first glow in bright red and pink, then in dark red with strips of white and yellow in between, and finally, as the sun disappears, they turn red and purplish. It is like a glimpse into heaven."

"What is that big red book you are reading?

"It's a bible, Angie."

"I didn't know that the bible was that thick. The one that we read in Religion class is much smaller."

"That is an edition for children. This one is for adults. Some day you can read all of it, but that is a lot of reading.

"Grandpa, do animals go to heaven?"

"Why are you asking?"

"Today in the library at school I saw a book called *Animal Heaven*. It almost looks like a bible, but it's not red."

"I never heard of such a title. Are you sure it did not say *Animal Haven,* without the *e* before the *a*?"

"I know it said *Heaven*."

"I would like to see that book. Why don't you check it out tomorrow and we'll see what it says. Did you ask your teacher if there is a heaven for animals?"

"I did but she suggested I ask you."

"Why me?"

"She said that grandpas usually know such things."

"What a wise woman! I hope that there is some kind of heaven for animals, some kind of state of happiness, especially for the ones who had to work so hard and the ones who were mistreated."

"How about tigers and lions and rattlesnakes and mosquitoes?"

"You are asking tough questions, young lady. Animals, no matter how big, no matter how small, cannot commit sins because they have no free will. They cannot become criminals because nature makes them act the way they do. They cannot help it. They attack when they are threatened, when they get frightened, or when they are hungry and know of no other way to obtain food but by killing. They cannot help it. We can. We can say 'NO' if we feel like killing because we have a free will. And yet, we do as the lions and the tigers do. Every time you eat a hot dog you support the killing of animals. But that does not make you evil."

Angie stared at the sky for a while and then she said: "I don't think I'll eat any more hot dogs."

Fred was so moved by this child's innocence that he almost cried. *She is so much like I am*, he thought. *I have never really felt comfortable eating meat.* "I hope that all animals will be rewarded for their suffering with some kind of happiness. If not, I will have to ask God some tough questions when I get there. Don't forget to bring me that book. I'll let you read something about Saint Francis. I bet that he believed in it."

"Who is Saint Francis?"

"You bring me the book and I will find something you can read about Saint Francis. I know that he loved honey bees."

"Does the bible tell us?"

"Not really. Over many years I have read almost every page of it. In one place it says that we don't know. There is this book in Bible called *Ecclesiastes*, a strange name. It was written long before Christ was born. Those books are called *The Old Testament*.

"I know. Like the story of the creation."

"I see that they teach you well. Here is this book called *Ecclesiastes*. In the third chapter it reads:

> For the lot of man and of the beast is one lot. Both have
> the same life-breath, and man has no advantage over
> the beast. ... Who knows if the life breath of the children
> of men (That is our soul.) goes upward and the
> life breath of beasts goes earthward?

"It clearly says: *Who knows?*"

"Why do they call animals *beasts*?"

"That's just an antiquated, an old word. Your teacher says that grandpas know those things. Even the writer of *Ecclesiastes* doesn't know. Don't forget to bring me that book tomorrow."

The phone rang which ended the conversation.

──── DEBORAH AND THE BEECH TREE ────

"We are all alone up here on this hill. It is so peaceful in your shade. My parents already climbed you when they were children. You are no longer the most photogenic father of the bygone forest but I have always admired you. Remember when the loggers wanted to fell you just because lightning had struck you? They felled all the common trees around you, but when they decided to cut you down, both Ruth and I protested because beech trees are extremely rare in this part of the world. Even Travis was upset about their intention. He wanted Angie and Eric to enjoy you. Dad had actually built a little tree house supported by your mighty branches. Since he was a friend of the owner of the sawmill, he managed to spare your life. It would have taken the loggers a whole week to cut you down.

"From the tree house we could overlook the entire valley. You have been home to many children. You are still home to many red squirrels because of your beechnuts which we also enjoyed after our lips had turned blue from the blueberries growing where the sunlight managed to fall through your majestic branches.

"I remember when that lightning hit you. It ripped a gush through your tall trunk, which resembles a pillar in a gothic cathedral. The lightning took a large branch with it but you remained standing tall, firm and proud. You kept on producing more nuts than the squirrels and we could eat. Felling you would have been a chore, and then, well then the picnickers from the cities would miss your shade in the summer, and the pilots of small planes would complain that they lost their orientation point. Bird watchers and deer watchers would have to look for new vista points, and I would lose a source of inspiration. In ancient times people believed that trees like you were inhabited by deities and you would have been considered a sanctuary. During cold winter nights the wind whispers in your ears like in a dream. She sings of spring, sunshine, and children playing under you.

"If I had children we also would spend time in your sanctuary and listen to the harmonies of the wind in your red leaf branches. Children? I, a mother? That will always be wishful thinking, but I hope that I can remain as strong as you did after misfortunes strike me. I sometimes sense them lurking behind bushes and at the horizon."

★★★

Isabel had sneakily followed Deborah. At one point she almost burst out laughing but controlled her emotions and uttered softly: "Oh my, oh my, yeigh, yeigh! Now she talks to a tree. Travis mentioned that she spends time up here. I had to find out what it is with this place. Thank God, she did not see me. Too bad, I could not make out what she was saying – damn! But now I know that she has gone crazy. I can't wait to tell Travis. This here is a splendid hiding spot behind these rocks. Next time Travis has to see this. For being a cripple, she walks briskly with her cane. Where are my cigarettes? Damn, I forgot them. Now I would really treasure one. I need a drink."

Part II

THE BUSY DREAMER

The evening after visiting her mighty beech tree, Deborah sat by the kitchen window sipping rosé wine and finally dozing off. She was up on the hill again sitting under the beech tree. The color of the wine matched that of the evening sky shining through the branches. The ear-breaking roar of a motorcycle on the road that passed by the house tore her out of her dream. She knew that had to be Billy again on his devilish machine. He practically lived on his Kawasaki delivering small automobile parts to repair shops whose owners always expected delivery within the hour. At times Deborah fantasized that she, too, could dash off like Billy. It was her inborn urge to move.

I am not going to sit here at home in the kitchen and pout till I am gray. I used to tell my ABC students that they were unemployable as long as they remained handicapped. Illiteracy is a handicap. Not to be able to speak the language of a gringo employer is also a handicap, but those sorts of handicaps can be overcome with hard work. Mine, on the other hand, is irreversible. I need something to make up for it if I want to be accepted and respected. I need to apply at more colleges and universities. That is easier said than done. Who is going to pay the tuition? I know that Mom and Pop will do what they can, but their means are limited and I feel that they have supported me long enough. It is time I stood on my own feet. I need financial aid like scholarships and loans. I hate to take advantage of my handicap but what choice do I have?

That means that whoever makes the decision at a university has to see me. Oh, how I hate this!

Deborah jumped up and limped to the typewriter in her bedroom to compose more letters to go with university applications. She almost knocked over a chair in the living room where Mary was mending Fred's socks. Fred happened to enter.

"Fred, she is still busy like a bee, never slows down."

"No, Mary, bees do slow down when they get tired. They can sit for hours in one spot meditating. Debbie has not reached that point yet. It'll come."

"She is making the rounds again teaching the ABCs to some of her former students. She feels bad for them because they were let down. This time, however, they pay her."

"Is that so? Well then her getting laid off may have been a blessing in disguise."

"Possibly because she will need money badly. I don't know if you noticed, but every evening she has been hitting the typewriter filling out application forms for colleges and universities. This morning she mailed six of them at the Post Office. She has her heart set on the University of San Francisco or the University of Santa Clara."

"Two private universities, both Jesuit run," Fred commented with concern. "We cannot afford the tuition at either of them."

"She is well aware of that and has applied for scholarships. With her 4.00 GPA from the community college and our limited income her chances should be good. And don't forget that she is Catholic."

"I don't know how much that still counts. It seems to me that the difference between Catholic universities and other private schools is getting wishy-washy, and don't forget that scholarships usually pay only a small portion. Now they are all under pressure to give scholarships to minorities rather than Catholics."

"Fred, if there is ever a minority, she is it."

"How would they know? Admissions would have to see her, and then there would be no way of knowing in which direction the pendulum might swing."

"She has already been to see several department Chairs, and we all know how well she verbalizes. She could sell them a used car for a new one."

"I must say Debbie is a go-getter."

"Fred, you need to teach her how to drive so that she can live at home and eliminate the dorm expense."

"Excellent suggestion. If she puts her mind to it, she can do that, too."

"That is how she survives," said Mary. "She won't need us much longer."

★★★

The following evening, Deborah went to see her sister.

"Good afternoon, Ruth. What are you doing?"

"I am spraying my roses. They are infested with aphids. What brings you here? I thought that you were at the University of Santa Clara today."

"I was there yesterday and today. They have a very beautiful campus. You should see their roses. I saw someone releasing dozens of ladybugs from a small container. They eat the eggs which aphids lay."

"Around this house and in June that would take a lot of ladybugs with a ferocious appetite. You did not come here to teach me about roses and ladybugs."

"No, I did not. I have great news for you. First of all, dad is giving me driving lessons. I already bought the *Rules of the Road* for the written exam."

"That is indeed good news. How are the lessons going?"

"Not bad because dad has a lot of patience. You know that in my right leg and foot I do not have the strength that I should have. The real good news is that I have been accepted at Santa Clara as a junior with a one-year full tuition scholarship. I found out at the Religious Studies Department today. I am so excited! I visited the Chair. He said that the letters would go out in a week or so. He asked me to keep it under my hood that he had let the cat out of the bag before the Admissions Office mailed the letters."

"Good news again. Have you told mom and dad yet?"

"Tonight."

"Why the Religious Studies Department?"

"I am going to major in Theology."

"Theology? What kind of a job can you get in Theology? Mom and dad are not going to be around forever, you know."

"I could teach Religion.'

"Another volunteer job."

"You know that I have been asking our pastor why in our Catholic Church women cannot be ordained even though women fill more pews than men do. I talked to a Jesuit in Religious Studies. He seems to have no theological problems with women's ordination, only logistical ones. He said that in 1970, in Czechoslovakia, several women were ordained by a diocesan bishop because of the shortage of priests under the communist regime. He believes those to be valid ordinations even though Rome has not approved of them. I cannot wait to take a course from him."

"If he teaches that, Rome and the traditionalists around here will see to it that he gets fired. That is the reality, my dear little sister."

"Maybe, but before that happens I want to take a course from him."

Ruth dropped her clippers. "Are you dreaming of becoming …? … Haven't you received enough rejections already?"

"I have solid arguments in my mind for women's ordination. They already have female students at some seminaries today."

"Debbie!"

"The day will come when you hear the first woman deacon preach."

"Debbie, did you hear what I said before? Stop dreaming and go after something more realistic. The day comes when you will have to support yourself. Think of your old age. Study to become a chemist or a medical technician in a lab."

"Never give up, never give up!" That is what I told a refugee from Vietnam. He was trying to get into a graduate program in Berkeley. He has the equivalent of an M.A. in Physics but he cannot obtain the papers to prove it. He cannot even prove that he graduated from high school. Universities in North Vietnam are not allowed to send transcripts to students who fled. While the war is still going on, schools in North Vietnam will not even grace him with a brief response. He is much worse off than I am."

"It seems so. Let's go inside and have some coffee."

God, they will never ordain her, and not just because she is a woman, Ruth thought as she heated the water while Deborah was helping Eric with his homework, dissecting sentences."

★★★

Mrs. Walsh was sitting in her favorite living room chair on this quiet late afternoon. She had just finished praying her daily rosary, a tradition that dated back to her maternal grandparents in Dublin, Ireland. Suddenly Deborah came waltzing into the house swinging her cane in a jovial mood. She had visited the U. of Santa Clara once more and one of the Jesuit faculty members in Religious Studies had treated her to a cup of coffee in the Jesuit dining room.

Her mother looked serious and said: "Debbie, sit down here, if you are capable of sitting still. We need to talk."

"Oh?"

"What is that I hear from Ruth? Are you dreaming of becoming a deacon or a priest?"

"I have felt the desire for quite some time."

"Are you totally out of your mind?"

"Why?"

"We raised you as a good Catholic. Don't you know that the church teaches that only men can be ordained? Did Christ have female apostles?"

"Mom, I am familiar with that argument, but there are very good arguments in favor of ordaining women as well."

"I don't want to hear them. Just keep in mind: Unless you accept all that the Catholic Church teaches, you are not a true Catholic."

"Mother, I do consider myself a true Catholic. When I challenge the hierarchy on certain traditions, I do it out of love for the church, to make it into a better church. The hierarchy is not infallible."

"Debbie, Debbie! Since when do you hold such liberal ideas? I worry about you."

REGISTRATION

Registration lines at the old gymnasium were long on this Friday in September of 1970. Only a few students were equipped with umbrellas. Deborah Walsh, having bought a rather large one at the campus store, one that said 'University of Santa Clara' on it in red and white, offered to share it with another student who expressed her appreciation but turned red in the face as she got a closer glimpse of Miss Walsh. Deborah, being used to such reactions, initiated the conversation.

"My name is Deborah Walsh. I am a transfer student."

"I am Edith Daring. Nice to meet you. I am a freshman, new in this area."

"Where are you from, if I may ask?"

"From Morgan Hill," answered Edith.

"Do you already know what you want to major in?" asked Deborah.

"No, I am undeclared, but I am leaning toward History and German. They have a new major in German and two new professors. I talked to one. He is from the University of Illinois, originally from Germany. He is cool. He has a sense of humor. My roommate had him last year. She says that initially he came across as being very strict but after a while he revealed himself as a person with a soft heart. I am going to sign up for his intermediate class. What is your major?"

"I have decided on Religious Studies and I just might end up in the same German class. I had three years of it in high school. Religious Studies majors have to pass a reading exam in a foreign language."

Finally the doors opened and there was much elbow pushing. Each academic department had its own registration table. Deborah headed straight for Religious Studies to make sure that she would get into the courses that she wanted. Fr. X. behind the table recognized her. He was the one who had given her the good news about the scholarship and he was the one who saw no fundamental problem with ordaining women.

"Do you still want to sign up for German?" Fr. X asked.

Deborah was stunned by that man's memory. "Yes, I do. I don't remember if I told you that it is my dream to read Karl Rahner some day."

"Lady, you are ambitious. Even native speakers have a hard time understanding his writings."

"Never give up, never give up," she said with a broad smile and headed for the Modern and Classical Language tables. To fill out the registration cards for German and Latin she had to squeeze in between two boys. One of them kept looking at her whenever she was not looking. Upon leaving the table he pushed his friend next to him, and he might have burst out laughing had he not covered his mouth with one hand. Deborah turned around and she noticed that he looked like a clean-cut boy wearing expensive clothes.

Both language courses were still open, as was Biology. That department was offering a course on bees and butterflies. Deborah felt that she could not pass that up. All she had to do after that was to walk to the campus store in the student union to purchase her textbooks with the money she had saved up from teaching the ABCs. In the book store she ran into Edith again and the two decided on a cup of coffee in the cafeteria.

"My treat," said Deborah. Leicester, who was a senior, soon joined them. Deborah noticed that this time Edith did not blush. She also noticed that Leicester kept his eyes glued on Edith while he drank his root beer. Something about her seemed to fascinate him. She was a blond with aquamarine eyes and aquamarine earrings. *He seems to be my age, late twenties,* thought Deborah, much older than Edith.

"Are you coming to the dance tonight?" he asked Edith. "I don't mean the freshmen dance. A group of us are meeting at a house at 425 Bellomy St. Three students, friends of mine, are renting that house. Lots of beer. You won't find beer at the freshmen dance."

"I really don't know. I am not into drinking."

"Come on now. We have to start off the semester right. They have a large living room with a hardwood floor, ideal for dancing."

"If you don't see me by 8:15, don't wait for me."

"You don't know what you are missing. I still hope to see you there." Before leaving, he turned to Deborah and asked, "… And you are?"

"I am Deborah Walsh, a new transfer student." At that, he left.

"What a jerk," remarked Edith. Care to see my dorm room in Swig Hall? It's a rather new dorm for freshmen."

"I would love to."

The lobby had comfortable furniture and on one wall hung the oil painting of Benjamin Swig who had done the fundraising for the dorm and pumped quite a bit of his own money into it. The rooms were small but cozy. Edith's roommate was one of those Berkeley flower children. She seemed very nice. Deborah had noticed again that Edith had not blushed when her roommate entered. On the way home she felt that she had found a true friend, eight years younger then she, but a friend nevertheless.

★★★

The semester went well and Deborah had found a counselor, the Jesuit professor of Dogmatic Theology whom students nicknamed "Father X" because he would always logically arrive at an answer like a mathematician arrived at the unknown value of x in a mathematical equation. Deborah knocked somewhat timidly on the professor's door that was half ajar.

"Hello, Miss Walsh. What can I do for you?"

"Fr. X., I came to ask you a very personal question, if I may."

"Go ahead. Have a seat. Do you want the door closed?"

"No, there will be no need for that. My question is: Do you pray the rosary?"

"Now, that is a personal question and a tricky one at that. If I say 'yes,' I am old- fashioned. If I say 'no,' I am a liberal. So, I'll just stick to the truth. Yes, I pray the rosary, but not necessarily every day."

"Why is that?"

"There are many forms of prayer and the rosary is just one of them. Why are you asking?"

"The other day I overheard a conversation in the cafeteria between four students who ridiculed the rosary as something outdated, a toy for old women. It bothered me a lot because I happen to like that form of prayer and I consider myself anything but old-fashioned."

"Your progressive and somewhat extreme views are no secret in this department. That is why I am both surprised and delighted that you value that type of prayer. Judgments like the ones by those four students do not surprise me. Sad to say, I have heard clergy belittle the rosary. Critics do not understand that the rosary is a meditative prayer which

59

is completely based on scripture. If the '*Hail Marys*' are rattled down mechanically without meditating on scripture, the 20 minutes become a monotonous recital that can put one to sleep, even though it never hurts to ask Mary frequently to pray for us. When I say the words '… and blessed is the fruit of thy womb, *Jesus*,' however, I visualize Jesus in particular scenes in the gospels. I am sure I am not telling anything new here, or am I?"

"No, you are not, but I have a problem staying with one and the same picture from scripture, let's say for example the presentation in the temple, for the entire duration of ten '*Hail Marys*.' I find that boring. That is why I cover all three mysteries, the Joyful, the Sorrowful, and the Glorious, with one rosary. I also make up my own because the three mysteries jump over Jesus' three years of public teaching as if they did not exist. They jump from Jesus' childhood straight to the crucifixion."

Fr. X. could not keep from laughing and said: "Wonderful solution. That's exactly what I do. It makes the rosary a lot more interesting. You should never feel bound by traditional formulas. Prayer is something personal between you and God, and the format that you feel comfortable with is pleasing to God. Naturally, where the rosary is prayed as a group prayer, there is no way around set formulas."

"Thanks, Father. I was hoping to receive that kind of affirmation."

"If you have no bigger problems in your religious life, consider yourself in fine shape."

"Oh, I do have others. I have a problem with calling Mary the Mother of God. God has no mother. We should call her the Mother of Jesus."

"Now that would get us to the Council of Ephesus in 431 when that term was created. Are you sure you want to get into that now?"

"No thanks, some other time maybe."

"Just think mathematically: 12 equals 10+2, but 12 also equals 6+6. Therefore, 10+2 equals 6+6. Right?"

"Right." Deborah could not keep from laughing. "You are putting me back into 4th grade."

"Okay, fourth grader: Mary is the mother of Jesus. Jesus is God. So, logically, she can be called Mother of God."

"You got me there. And yet, I would argue that Mary is the mother of Jesus only in as far as he is human."

"Miss Walsh, you are too smart for your age. That gets us to a different topic before you run off like a busy bee. The Graduate Theological Union in Berkeley is offering a three-day seminar for students in Theology. The topic is: *The Second Vatican Council and its projected impact on the liturgy in the Catholic Church."* Would you be interested?"

"Would I? Of course I would, but how much does it cost?"

"Our department has a fund to subsidize registration and the Jesuit community is making financial aid for room and board available. I think that you would be an excellent candidate. If you are interested, swing by the secretary to pick up an application form for the registration and then go to the Jesuit residence to pick up another application for room and board. Feel free to list me as a reference. You'll need two from this department."

"I don't know what to say. Thank you, Father."

"It is always a pleasure to talk to a free spirited mind like you. I am glad you brought your umbrella. It's pouring out there."

"I like rain. Bye Father."

"Bye, Miss Walsh."

THE BABY SHOWER

Deborah had one hour to kill until Ruth would come to pick her up for the ride to Berkeley. She decided to leave a note for her mother who was attending her weekly Friday morning mass.

Dear Mom,

By the time you come back from church we will have left for the Graduate Theological Union. I'll check into one of the dorms and then we will spend the afternoon touring the University of California campus. Ruth wants to see it.

Yesterday at breakfast you asked me how the baby shower had gone. With Ernie's unexpected visit, I never got a chance to tell you.

A week has already passed since. The shower was for Stephanie Gallion. She is due in one month. I had planned to go with five other girls, who all went, but the final announcement as to the exact date and time arrived in my mailbox a few days late. I had bought a neat little chiffon dress and a colorful baby blanket because they know that it is a girl. It was actually more than I could afford but that's what a credit card is for.

On Sunday, Sue, one of my classmates, noticed me sitting in the cafeteria all by myself. She came over and said: "Deborah, we missed you at the shower. ... What's wrong? You look so down."

"What's wrong?" I answered. "I did not receive the final announcement about the date and the time until the day after."

"How come? Everyone else received hers already on Thursday."

"So I heard."

She jumped on the defensive. "You are not accusing us of ...!"

"No, I am not accusing anyone," I quickly answered. Then I added: "Mail service has been somewhat unreliable lately."

Sue explained that she and Karen had taken the mail to the post office and that she saw how Karen dropped the whole pack of letters into the drop box. I was not blaming anyone at that point but now I have reasons to be suspicious because Sue immediately jumped on the defensive, and none of my classmates said anything to me the day before, something like: "See you at the shower." Finally, today, I saw Karen in the cafeteria. She also saw me but she quickly turned around and pretended not to have seen me.

Mom, I should not dwell on happenings like these. I ought to be used to that by now. Mom, am I paranoid? The mail service has been poor lately, as you well know. Today I went to visit the young couple, Wayne and Stephanie, to deliver the presents. They are my age, friendly and welcoming. They already picked a name for the baby: Julia. They liked the dress and the blanket and we had coffee and leftover cake. But then I received another blowing reminder, at no fault of theirs. They have a four-year-old boy, Nick, who blares out everything that puzzles him. Stephanie had gone to the kitchen and Nick had followed her. With the door half open, Wayne and I heard him asking: "Mom, how come she has such a funny face? She looks goofy." All Wayne could say, as he turned red, was: "I am sorry." Stephanie came back to the table and apologized and Wayne took Nick to his bedroom where they seemed to have a long talk.

Have I gotten overly sensitive like blind people who no longer want to called "blind" but "vision impaired" or "visually challenged"? The fact is that I do look goofy. Mom, don't tell dad anything about this because this always hurts him more than it does me. Tell him that I received an "A" on my term paper in Dogmatic Theology, in spite of the fact that I disagreed with Fr. M. on certain aspects of Ordination and the Eucharist. He is a tough grader but his comments seem to indicate that he appreciated my form of argumentation. You know that I am not like a parrot who simply echoes what he has been taught. Now I want to read Fr. M's manuscript on marriage. I had told him earlier that I would like to. Maybe that drop of honey got me the "A". I'll call you from Berkeley.

Love, Debbie

★★★

Spring had entered early this year in the Bay Area. The blossoms of the citrus and peach trees had turned radiant in the sunlight and the bees were loading up with nectar and pollen. Likewise, Deborah felt that she was entering a new phase in her life. As she sat on the bench under a giant maple tree next to one of the buildings of Berkeley's Theological Union, Linda, another conference participant, joined her.

"That was a refreshing and uplifting presentation," said Linda. "The speaker combined a very serious topic with a genuine sense of humor."

"I was surprised about her straightforwardness because I think that she is treading on thin ice," added Deborah. "She is apt to lose her teaching position."

"Do you disagree with her?"

"No, not at all," Deborah answered with emphasis. "She only confirmed what I have felt for some time now. Why do you have to be born male to image Christ? Mary is a mediatrix, and so are all the female saints. Why do we have to die first to play that role, when men are allowed to play that role as priests here on earth?"

"I never heard of that argument before, but I like it. I would love to study for ordination." Linda blushed a little when she said that.

"Me, too," answered Deborah. "I feel the calling, but you know that the hierarchy is a men's club. They probably feel that a woman is not cut out to walk in the apostles' shoes."

"I don't think that is the decisive reason for their attitude. It is a psychological thing. To have a woman in vestments standing next to them at the altar, or kissing the ring of a woman with miter and staff? Think of it. How would you feel as a man having been brought up in a tradition such as ours? Tradition has shaped them. It's just like the wide-spread notion that females are not cut out for science and engineering."

It was sheer coincidence that not far from where they were sitting they could hear two male students with their reaction to that same presentation making fun of the presenter. "Man, if that happens we are done in. I could not see myself as an associate pastor under a woman pastor telling me what I can and cannot do. You know that women have a tendency to take over."

"Worse than that. What kind of a man would go to a woman for confession? Jesus was wise not to choose women apostles. We could not even live in the same rectory." The rest of the conversation the girls could not make out because the wind had shifted direction.

"You see what I said?" asked Linda. "We are dealing with a psychological barrier of two machos, not a theological one. When God made man she was still practicing."

Deborah laughed out loud. "And yet," she answered, "men can be such wonderful fathers who love and respect their daughters, like mine does. I wish the wind were blowing in our direction to pick up more of their conversation."

"Deborah, the wind is going to blow in the other direction for years to come."

"Well put, Linda. Those two will probably be ordained and, God forbid, one of them might even become a bishop."

"It is time for the discussion. Let's see if those two machos are going to be there. Don't be timid!"

"Deborah, I am glad we met. Let's have lunch together some day."

"Right on!"

Unfortunately, lunch never materialized because Linda was called home on a family emergency due to which the two never exchanged addresses and phone numbers. They had not even bothered to mention each other's last name.

EDITH AND DEBORAH

The lounge in Swig Hall was unusually quiet on Memorial Day in 1971. Edith and Deborah had planned to go out for lunch. Later in the afternoon they were going to attend a German Club meeting at which one of the professors of German was going to show the movie *Death in Venice* which Deborah had always wanted to see ever since she had read the translation of that novella by Thomas Mann. Before that, between 2:00 and 4:00, Deborah wanted to put in two hours shelving books in the library. As Edith stepped off the elevator, Deborah was ready to rush to the restaurant not to be late for the library.

"Wait a minute. We have plenty of time to kill," said Edith. "Let's sit here for a minute and relax. You are always so hyper." She grabbed Deborah by one arm and pushed her into one of the easy chairs. "You are always running," she said.

"I know I haven't relaxed lately."

"Debbie, you worry me. I am telling you this as your best friend. You have gotten yourself involved in too many activities. You are busier than a bee. You are killing yourself. In summer, a working bee lasts only four to five weeks.

Deborah felt that it was nice of Edith to call her Debbie. Normally only her own family did.

"You are beginning to sound just like my mother but don't forget that I am eight years older than you and my years after community college have not been very productive. I need to make up for lost time."

"I was not suggesting that you become a couch potato but, for heaven's sake, give yourself some time to breathe, to relax, and to meditate. Everybody needs that."

"I meditate in bed. I meditate under my favorite beech tree. I meditate on the porch watching our bees and the sunset."

"It seems that those bees have hypnotized you. You have become just like them."

"I love'em and they recognize me. Haven't been stung all spring."

"I still say that you need to slow down. You are involved with the Chaplin's Office; you are part of the liturgy committee; you are the leader of a bible study group; you work in the language lab; you re-shelve books in the library; and you teach the ABCs; and who knows what else … Superwoman!"

"I admit, you are right. I need to step on the brakes. Let's go and enjoy our lunch now."

Edith pulled her back into the chair. "Wait a minute. You want to run again. I have been wanting to ask you a very personal question."

"So, what's that?"

"You are adopted. Right?"

"Yes, I am. How did you know?"

"You mentioned it to one of your classmates and she told me."

"Gossipers."

"Do you know anything about your biological parents?"

Deborah hesitated with her answer and Edith took her by the hand and said: "You can confide in me. I am also adopted. You can tell me."

"Well, what do you know?"

"Why don't you tell me your story now and later, at the restaurant, I'll tell you mine.

Deborah studied Edith's curious expression and asked: "Why in the world did we hide that from each other. Are we normal?"

"I think we are," answered Edith, "but we are not the common types. We differ in more than one way. Come on, let's hear it."

"Alright. There is not much I know because I was only three years old when the Walshes adopted me. I have no recollection of my father. He served in the Air Force toward the end of World War II, and in March of 1944, during one of the many air strikes he was shot down over Cologne, Germany. I had just turned one.

"As far as my mother, I only remember her sitting on a bed one day, crying and holding me tight. I didn't know why she was crying. Maybe, it was after she lost her job at a bank and had no means to support herself and me. My adoptive parents told me that we lived in Alviso, right north of Santa Clara and San Jose, at the southern tip of the Bay. I found out that she died at O'Connor Hospital in San Jose of lung cancer when I was three. Asking around Alviso when I was in high school, I found a couple who remembered us. In fact, they had a family photo of us which they gave me to keep. It shows my dad in his Air Force uniform and me at the age of one on my mother's lap. On the back someone had written *The Gellhorn Family, 1944.* All the couple remembered was that my father had been a fireman and that my mother loved nature and tended a beautiful flower garden, and that she was always reading. They confirmed what my adoptive parents had told me, that I had no siblings and that my parents originally had come from Los Angeles. They had no knowledge of any relatives. They remembered that my mother died at O'Connor Hospital of lung cancer, and the Walshes, who adopted me, told me that I was taken to an orphanage before my mother was taken to the hospital, and that they adopted me a few weeks after my mother died. Many times I have pictured my mother in my mind, her sitting on the hospital bed crying and missing me. I guard the only family picture like a treasure.

"The Walshes had a daughter by the name of Ruth who accepted me like a blood sister. We have always felt close. That is it in a nutshell. Now let's run to the restaurant because I want to be at the library at 2:00."

"Run? We are walking."

"Alright, I realize that I should slow down. My family calls me "Busy Bee.""

Edith was not sure that Deborah really meant what she just said, but she made sure that they walked leisurely. In some article on Character Development she had read that it is very rare that after the age of 20 a person will change significantly.

Edith made sure that the 10-minute walk took 20 minutes. There wasn't the slightest breeze in the air. They stopped for a little while to observe a couple of butterflies on a flowery bush on someone's front lawn. Deborah noted that butterflies take forever to drink. "They seem to be completely oblivious to the world around them while they drink."

"Completely oblivious," Edith repeated, and suddenly the two realized that they were holding hands.

★★★

They liked the little restaurant on Park Ave. because of its elegance and décor and because the portions were reasonable, preventing waste of food. The waitresses did not usher you out as quickly as possible by plopping the bill by your plate before you even started the dessert. Deborah had once stated in an art class that for her the décor of a restaurant was as important as the food itself. Some of her classmates who only knew cafeterias and hamburger joints thought that she was nuts.

While they were sipping their second lemonade, Deborah reminded Edith that it was her turn now to summarize her story.

"If you promise me not to want to run off after five minutes."

"Promise."

"Well, then. How should I start? I was born in a jail in 1952, a Hungarian jail near the Austrian border. I wish I knew the name of our hometown, presumably in the same district as the jail. My father, Joseph Czaba, was a forester. My mother, Mia Czaba, who was never afraid of anything, had been fired as a newspaper columnist because of her criticism of the Moscow oriented politics of the town's mayor and certain communist party leaders. She stood for independence from Moscow. At a birthday party, after a glass of whisky and a glass of wine, she had referred to Josef Stalin as a *vicious bloodhound* without knowing everyone present at the party. The next day she was arrested and sentenced to one year of hard labor in a labor camp.

Pressed for time, my father could not find a defense lawyer with enough courage to defend her. Otherwise she may have gotten away with a lighter sentence on account of the fact that I was already five months old in her womb. After the prison doctor determined that she was indeed five months pregnant, the prison staff tried to talk her into an abortion arguing that hard labor would result in a miscarriage anyway, but my mother vehemently refused."

"What a courageous woman she must have been!"

"She was. Otherwise I would not be here. There must have been an administrator with feelings because soon thereafter my mother was transferred to a regular jail. Three months later disaster struck again. I was born but my mother was not allowed to see me."

"No! – Why? What happened?"

"Party officials had decided that she would be an unfit mother because of her subversive political viewpoints. They had me transferred to a government orphanage and refused to identify it. That leads us into the second phase of the drama."

Edith noticed that Deborah was not looking at her watch. So she continued: "After one month or so, my dad somehow found out to which orphanage I had been transferred. At the same time he also heard that the same orphanage was looking for a new janitor. He promptly went to the authorities and asked to be released from his job as a forester because of frequent chest pains. His family physician, whom he trusted, had courageously written up a brief statement indicating serious heart problems. He said to him jokingly: 'You have the heart of a bull. That is serious.' The authorities released him from his job as a forester, which was a low level government position. My dad then went to the orphanage applying for the janitorial job and was hired. Now he got to see me every day, but he was extremely careful not to identify himself as the father. His mind could not put up with that forever. What if some day, his daughter were to get adopted by a family? While my mother was still in jail, he managed to kidnap me during his night shift and carry me out of the orphanage in a trash bin."

"My God! What would have happened if you had started to cry?"

"Well, I did not. That must have been divine intervention."

"Maybe, or he muffled you."

"Could be. My mother never became a suspect in the kidnapping because she was still confined in jail with very limited contact to the outside world, barring one weekly supervised visit from my dad. At the orphanage my dad had faked great shock when he heard of the disappearance of a baby from the orphanage. Rumor had already spread that there were hoodlums in Europe who took large sums of money from wealthy couples who were desperately looking for babies to adopt.

"My dad had taken me to his sister, Rosa Czaba, who lived alongside a large forest bordering on Austria. One day, when he visited my mother, the supervising guard stepped out for a few minutes, and my dad broke the news to my mother. She wisely managed to suppress tears so as not to alert the returning guard."

"I can't believe it!" exclaimed Deborah, and all the heads around them turned.

"You better believe it. We have been sitting here taking up table space for a long time. Shouldn't we continue the odyssey elsewhere?"

"We better. How about a shady bench in the Rose Garden?"

"Good idea. Let's pay and go."

Edith was pleasantly surprised that her "busy bee" friend agreed to listen to the next half hour of the ordeal. Both were fond of roses, and they found a shady spot with an excellent view of a variety of rose bushes.

"Now, if you are ready for it, here comes the third act of the drama: The year was up, and my mother was released from jail. She had been a clever actress making the jail authorities believe that they had successfully brainwashed her from her stupid western ideas. Naturally, she spent half of her time at Rosa's, her sister-in-law's house. Neighbors and friends knew that I had been removed from her but did not know about my whereabouts.

"One foggy evening, my mother gave me a mild sleeping pill, wrapped me up warm, and stuck me into a wicker basket. My parents packed important papers and photos and a supply of clothing into two large backpacks and, upon darkness, worked their way through dense forest in the direction of Austria. Since my dad had been a forester in that area he knew every corner of that forest.

"By 5:00 a.m. they reached the end of the forest and, suddenly, they heard men's voices which my dad identified as voices of the border patrol. Mom and dad instinctively hid behind and under dense bushes. After a while the voices could no longer be heard. Mom and dad crawled out of their hiding places and noticed that they had ants crawling all over them. Brushing themselves off, dad sarcastically whispered: 'Those are Hungarian ants. Good riddance!' Luckily, none had gotten into the wicker basket.

"The forest cleared and dawn was already making it risky to go on, but they did. They finally crossed the dividing road spotting no border patrol. They managed to roll under a barbed wire fence onto a cow meadow. They had reached Austria. On the long walk to the nearest farm house I began to cry and my mother freed me from the wicker basket."

"That is a heart-breaking story," remarked Deborah. She looked at her watch and said: "I am late for the library."

Edith grabbed her by the arm. "The shelving of books can wait until tomorrow. There are five parts to my adoption story. We have covered only three."

"I think you are right. Let's hear the other two."

"Well, around 1952, the beginning of the so called *economic miracle*, Germany and Austria were in dire need of foreign workers because many men had lost their lives, were still missing in Russia, or had become invalids. My dad, knowing some German, soon found employment at a sawmill 10 kilometers outside of Vienna. We had two rooms in the house of a retired nurse who gave my mother daily lessons in German. My dad managed to buy an old army motorcycle to make commuting to work easier. One frosty evening in January of 1953 it was already dark and there was black ice on the road. He was wearing his helmet alright, but an oncoming truck, not aware of the black ice, was unable to stop on time and knocked my dad off his motor cycle against a telephone pole. My dad died that night in a small hospital from head injuries while my mother was with him holding his hands and praying with him."

"Edith, you should write up your story for *Readers Digest* or make it into a historical novel. It would sell."

"Let me get through college first. Care to hear act five?"

"Yes, I wanted to hear why and how you were adopted."

"Well then. One day my mother decided to emigrate to the United States. In high school in Hungary she had taken four years of English before Russian became a requirement for all. She went to the U.S. consulate in Vienna to apply for immigrant visas and was told that we needed a sponsor. She was lucky, because after WWII, during the American occupation of Austria, there seems to have been a romantic involvement between our landlady the nurse, and one of the American soldiers, a Mr. Bill Daring, who by 1954 owned a small farm outside of Gilroy where he grew artichokes and garlic. Although he was married to a nice lady by the name of Rita, he and our landlady still exchanged greetings on birthdays and at Christmas. Our landlady put in a good word for us, and since Bill needed workers, he sponsored us. I don't know how my mother was able to come up with the money for that long trip by ship and by train to California.

"Bill and Rita Daring liked us a lot, and instead of sending my mother into the fields he put her in charge of their large vegetable and flower garden, a job which she really enjoyed. When I was six, however, my mother was sick a lot and was finally diagnosed with cancer of the pancreas and died half a year later. Bill and Rita Daring liked me a lot. They had no children of their own and decided to adopt me. Edith Czaba became Edith Daring."

"A name that fits your character."

"Thanks a lot. Like yours, my adoptive parents have been extremely nice to me, but I always keep a photo of my birth parents on the wall over my desk in Swig Hall."

"Edith, I am smitten. Tell me something. How do you know all these details? You were only six at the time your mother died."

"She told me the story many times, and during her illness she shared many details with the Darings. Up to the age of six I grew up bi-lingual, and my mother left me Hungarian readers used in the lower grades, little stories which I literally devoured as a kid. That made it possible for my aunt Rosa to correspond with me. She still writes to me and occasionally digs up the past."

"Edith, I find it very strange that, as close as we have become, it took us a year to share our stories. Strange. We *are* a different breed."

Leaving the Rose Garden Edith finally answered: "Yes, Debbie, we are queer and one of a kind. If we run, you can still get in half an hour at the library."

"No, Edith. This time I choose to be different. Tomorrow is another day. Let's just walk leisurely and watch those butterflies again and be in time for "Death in Venice." Edith could not believe what she heard and was now convinced that she had a mission.

DEBORAH AND LEICESTER

"Hi, Leicester. May I join you? I need to sit down and relax for a while."

Leicester looked around to see if anyone was looking, even after one year of knowing Deborah. Spring had once again made its entry into the Bay Area and the cafeteria was almost empty this Sunday afternoon. "Of course, Deborah, you may. How are your courses this quarter?"

"My courses are fine, but with the overload that I am carrying, there is little time to rest or socialize."

"Socialize? Would you care to come to a movie with me tonight, let's say around 7:00?"

"I would love to. I almost never get invited. But it's Sunday and I haven't been to church yet. I would like to attend the 7 o'clock mass in the mission church. That's why I decided to stay on campus after working in the library up to now."

"I understand. I am a Baptist by upbringing. I haven't gone either but we don't have a Sunday evening service."

"You are most welcome to join me as a guest."

"Oh no, I would not know what to do there."

"You don't have to do anything. Just watch us, and then tell me what you think. How about it?"

"Thanks for the invitation, maybe some other time. I am not that much of a churchgoer anymore but I do have a question for you. I hear that for you Catholics the consecration and communion are the most important parts of the mass. Do you actually believe that your priests have the power to transform bread and wine into Christ's body and blood? What do you call that again? Trans … something."

"Transubstantiation."

"If you believe that, then you actually believe that you are eating the body of Jesus and drinking his blood. Isn't that cannibalism? Doesn't that make you cannibals?"

They looked at each other for quite a while. Then Deborah admitted: "That is a tough one because there is nothing wrong with your logic. And yet, if you would understand biblical symbolism you would see that we are no cannibals. When Jesus says: 'He who eats my flesh and drinks my blood has life eternal' – I believe it's John, chapter 6 -- He is saying that the person who accepts him fully, without reservation, the whole Jesus, will have eternal life because Jesus *is* eternal life. When we eat the consecrated bread and drink the consecrated wine we are not eating flesh and we are not drinking blood in a biological sense. Biologically we are eating bread and drinking wine. We eat his body *in the form of bread* and we drink his blood *in the form of wine*. Doing so, the risen Christ with his glorified body becomes one with us in a very special way. I don't think that you can call that cannibalism. It is a spiritual union with the risen, glorified Christ.

On a physical level, you can parallel that union with the union of a mother and a baby in her womb. ... Puzzled? ... Shocked?"

"I never heard that kind of an explanation before. In our church we do not believe in the transformation of bread and wine. For us, the reception of the bread is a mere commemoration of the Last Supper."

"Well, you are at one end of the spectrum and we are at the other. Martin Luther proposed a nice compromise: It is called 'consubstantiation', which means that Jesus becomes present not *in the form* of bread and wine but *with* bread and wine. I consider both frail attempts at explaining a mystery which we cannot fully understand. What is important is that we believe in the real union. *With* or *in the form of*, what's the practical difference?"

"You seem to know a lot. Excellent Sunday School?"

"Oh, no. Transubstantiation and consubstantiation are not material for Sunday School. Theology happens to be my major."

"For some reason I thought that you were in Elementary Education. Didn't you teach reading and writing?"

"Yes, I did, at a public library, but that program got canceled."

"What can you do with a major in Theology?"

"I can teach Religion. You might also be in for a surprise some day when you see me as a deacon behind the altar."

"You know that they don't ordain women in your church. In ours they don't either."

"You are right. They don't. They also once believed that the earth was the center of the universe and they condemned Galileo Galilei for teaching otherwise. Now they know better. We need more popes like John XXIII."

"You in vestments behind the altar? In that case I would accept your invitation."

"Leicester, at the beginning of our conversation you stated that you are not much of a churchgoer anymore. Why is that?"

"I don't have the time. I carry a heavy course load."

"If you were to add up the number of weekend hours you spend in watching ball games and movies on TV, hours you spend on Friday nights at beer parties, and the hours you spend daydreaming, how many hours would that come to per week?"

"That's hard to say. Maybe 20. A man needs to have some fun."

"I really respect your honesty, Leicester. It takes courage to be honest. Now imagine you die and God asks you how many hours you devoted to Him in church every week and you answer, 'I couldn't go because I had too much homework and I needed to have some fun.' How well do you think that might go over?"

She really likes to wedge people into a corner, he thought, and at that point several students came in and sat at a table near him and Deborah. What a godsent!

"I have to go now, preacher. I just remembered that I am supposed to do a lab project in Chemistry today," Leicester said suddenly and quietly. "As always, it was very nice talking to you. Each time I learn something new. Let's meet again some day when we have more time and some privacy," he added softly and left.

Deborah finished her coffee by herself. She sat there looking at his cup. It was still half full. *He really isn't a bad guy. Maybe I preach too much, but I think that he'll be back.*

★★★

Surely enough, a few days later Leicester was back. He was looking around in the cafeteria to see if Deborah had responded to his phone call. He found her, punctual as always, sitting in some secluded corner, just the way he liked it.

"Hi, Deborah, I'm glad you could make it. As I told you on the phone, I could use your input on something. It's rather urgent."

"I feel flattered, Leicester. It is rare that fellow students ask me for help. What kind of input are we talking about?"

"First, can I get you something? A coke, fruit juice, coffee?"

"Coffee with cream would be fine."

Deborah noticed that on the way to the coffee bar he looked around as if to be sure nobody was watching. *I really have to stop imagining things. I have to get over this paranoia. I also need to cut back on all that coffee. It isn't healthy.* By the time she could yell to Leicester that she was changing the order to fruit juice, he had already filled the coffee cups.

"Here we are." Leicester spilled some of his coffee as he handed Deborah hers. He thought of his wife who always reprimanded him for overfilling the cups. There never was enough room left for the cream.

"What's with your wristwatch, Deborah?"

"The glass is cracked but the watch runs fine. My dad gave it to me for my 21st birthday. It's a self-winding Omega watch."

"Listen, my brother-in-law is a watch repairman. He can replace the crystal. I can take it to him tomorrow in return for your help."

"Thanks. That's very kind of you. Take it, but tell me how the movie was last night."

"You would have liked it. None of those cheap thrillers or comedies."

"As I told you, I hadn't been to church yet. But now, tell me why we are here."

"Well, you see, I am enrolled in this Art History class and we are supposed to write an interpretation of an art work of our own choosing. It has to express despair and frustration. We just covered Expressionism and New Realism during and after World War I, but the artwork does not have to be from that time. He goes by themes. Next time it might be happiness or melancholy. I found this picture of Mary, mother of Jesus. It is a photo of a sculpture that my mother took years ago on a tour through Europe. It looks like some sculptures by Rodin. Prof. Hein never saw it. We don't know who the artist is, but he approved it for my paper. It is due tomorrow morning at 8:00."

"That gives you little time. Not enough to write a first class paper. How can I help you?"

"This picture puzzles me, and I thought that since you major in Theology, you might be able to give me some good ideas for my paper. The sculpture portrays Mary in a most horrible way while all other statues and paintings of her that I have seen portray her as a rather sweet and beautiful woman. The artist plunged an arrow into her side, and her face is a mask of despair, distorted by pain, like screaming in agony. Just gruesome. Why? Nobody shot an arrow into her. Nobody tortured her. Underneath it says MATER DOLOROSA, whatever that means."

Deborah looked at him sort of puzzled but with a smile. *He cannot be too smart if he has never heard of MATER DOLOROSA.* Not getting any verbal response from her, Leicester went on, saying: "Don't you call her *full of grace* and *blessed art Thou among women*? She had it made."

"Fairly good coffee," said Deborah.

"Good coffee!" repeated Leicester, raising his voice. Were you listening to what I said before? This paper is due tomorrow morning at 8 o'clock. I need your help. I cannot now select another work of art. Selections need to be approved. I am stuck with this one."

"Why in the world did you wait until the night before? You should have skipped the movie last night. You'll be up until 4 o'clock tomorrow morning. That is really dumb! It might also be a lot easier if we knew the name of the artist, but I can tell you how I see this sculpture. You'll need to endure my explanation for 10 minutes."

Leicester was so frustrated that he answered, "I promise!" He really sounded desperate.

"Alright then. I know that you are married and that you are about my age, and you and Liz have a seven-year-old daughter named Jessica. Once you told me that you had always wanted a daughter. You love her so much that you would give your life for her. Right?"

"I would."

"Now let's move ahead on the scale of time. Jessica has now become a very well known 33-year old lady with a circle of friends who goes around teaching and helping a lot of people. Your love for her has not diminished. She is still your little daughter."

"What are you driving at?"

"Now let's say you live in a dictatorship where a judge can sentence you at will. Your daughter, a popular figure by now, has jealous enemies who denounce her. Any mishap in her life hurts you as much as it hurts her, even more. She is falsely accused of having committed certain crimes. A judge, who cannot find any wrong in her, wants to please the accusers and turns her over to them and their judge for judgment, knowing well that they might impose the death penalty. He washes his hands as if to say: 'I have nothing to do with the case. It's in your hands.' The guards won't let you nor Liz get near the jail but word has leaked out that they have whipped her and pushed a crown with thorns down on her head every time she refuses to answer a question."

"Wait a minute. I would never let that happen. I would storm in there with a baseball bat."

"That shows how much you love her, but you would never be let near that place and both you and Liz would suffer unparalleled agony. But wait, it gets worse. Execution has been set for some time in the afternoon and everybody knows the road up to a hill on which prisoners are led for the execution which is by hanging on a cross beam. Crowds gather and you are also standing at the road in hopes of getting close to her to hug her once more and cry with her. The procession slowly arrives and there are two others with your daughter meeting the same fate. All three are made to carry their own cross beam."

"Stop, I know what you are getting at."

"It gets worse but, obviously, I don't have to go into further details, except for one more thing: You are standing at a distance from the cross on which she is suffering a painful death. She sees you looking at her and her eyes are glued to yours, and there is nothing you can do for her. Would that not distort your face in psychological agony?"

"I get the picture. You have a very drastic way of putting me into Mary's sandals. Woman! Did you need to put it on that thick? You are worse than Rodin."

"That's what you get for waiting till the last minute with the paper."

"Do you think that the artist played that out in his mind?"

"He must have. Why, otherwise, would Mary's face be so distorted? The fact that 33 years earlier Mary had to give birth to her son in a stable, and that soon thereafter the family had to flee to Egypt as political refugees in order to escape the assassins of King Herod, was nothing in comparison to this. Yes, Mary was privileged, but I doubt that before Pentecost, before the Holy Spirit enlightened her and the apostles, she fully understood that her son was actually God himself in the form of a human being, nor did the apostles. None of those thousands of pictures of Mary, which portray her like a grown porcelain doll or like an immaculate beauty queen, are true to reality. That kind of art is called *kitsch*."

"That is strong wording but I can use it for my paper."

"Why did I give you these horrifying details? Generally, Christians do not place themselves into Mary's sandals and relive her passion. For them a picture like this one is just an ugly portrait or sculpture. To understand a realistic work of art like this one you have to get emotionally involved. Theology can be very rationalistic, like philosophy, but artists are no rationalists."

"Wait a minute. That is cool. Would you repeat that last statement so I can write it down?"

"Okay, write it down. I'll say it slowly: To understand an emotional work of art or a work of extreme realism like this one, the observer has to get emotionally involved and try to identify with the characters because artists are never as rational as philosophers and theologians can be. In this case, the observers have to put themselves into Mary's sandals and relive the passion. Otherwise they see this as nothing but an ugly portrait."

"That is cool. I'd better run to my room and strike the iron while it is hot. Thanks Deborah. You are smarter than our minister."

"Never mind your minister. You yourself were not so smart by waiting with this until curtain time. By the way, MATER DOLOROSA means GRIEF-STRICKEN MOTHER."

As Deborah was still sitting there seeing him dash off, she pondered over his last sentence. *"That is cool ... while the iron is hot."* A nice juxtaposition, she thought. She was getting to like him in spite of his faults and his mere average I.Q. *There is something about him that appeals to me. He is honest, but most of all, he came to a woman for advice, and not only that. He came to someone like me.*

MÉLISSA

In my previous life my face was distorted. It had turned downright ugly, in fact, because of inconsiderate humans who sprayed fruit trees in the hopes of killing insects. It hurt when some of my own sisters shied away from me. They would not understand my agony. Do I forgive them? Of course. Only someone who has experienced being "apis dolorosa" can understand the pain of rejection.

Who knows how I might have reacted if it had been some other bee who made me feel uneasy in her presence because of her looks?

We are not perfect either. In the human race men play lord over women in many areas. We do the same or worse except that with us it is the other way around. Come September, we kick all of our roly-poly brothers out of the beehive because they are no longer needed. We just kick them out and let them starve to death. How much meaner can you be?

═══ CONVERSATION WITH FATHER X. ═══

"Fr. X., I hope I am not disturbing. I can come back later."

"No, Miss Walsh, you are not disturbing. I need to take a break from grading these tests on the Pentateuch, the so-called Books of Moses. It is quite evident that half the class read the assigned pages with little attention to detail. Nowadays they call it speed-reading. Spring Quarter exams are around the corner. After they get this test back you'll see a good number of them praying in the mission church. I notice that at the end of every Quarter, right before finals. Now, Miss Walsh, what draws you back to this office?" Seeing that Fr. X was in a bad mood, Deborah was hesitant to take up his time, but then she reconsidered.

"I keep coming back to you because you always answer my questions clearly and to the point."

"Miss Walsh, to answer a question clearly and to the point is not always easy in theology, impossible at times, because there is a lot that our human mind cannot fully comprehend."

"Well, if some of the other professors don't have an answer, why not admit it instead of beating around the bush?"

"Good point, but at times you may be dealing with professional pride. Now, what kind of a question might you have up your sleeve today? You are graduating in a few weeks, aren't you?"

"Sure am. Can't wait, and yet, I'll miss Santa Clara."

"That's a good sign, and coming from you, I think it is a good grade for Santa Clara. What are your plans for after graduation?"

"Remember. Two years ago, before entering the university, we discussed women's ordination."

"You never give up, do you?"

"Nope, this topic has been on my mind ever since. You said at that time that you had no theological problem with women as priests, only logistical ones. Have you never gotten into trouble with the hierarchy over that?"

"Not yet because only lately has the topic come up. We haven't had much open theological discussion about it, but now that in the Episcopalian and Anglican churches they have begun to ordain women, discussion can only be around the corner."

"I've thought of a theological argument we could use with the ultra-conservatives in favor of women ordination."

"Oh? Let me hear it."

"The Catholic Church, always so afraid of change, teaches that Mary, the Blessed Mother, is a mediator. Besides praying to her to intercede for us, our church also encourage us to pray to other saints to intercede for us, making no distinction between male and female saints. The church also teaches that a priest is a mediator between us and Christ, especially when administering the sacraments. Right?"

"Right."

"Why then can a female be a mediator only after she dies while a man can fulfill that role while his heart is still beating?"

"Not a bad argument, Miss Walsh. Why are females only looked upon as mediators after they are dead and have been canonized? Men have a chance to be called to ordination, which means to be mediators, whereas women have to die first. Whether only ordained or canonized persons should be seen as mediators between us and God is, however, an entirely different question. I pray to my parents to intercede for me. We all become mediators when praying for others."

Deborah's thoughts were running ahead of Fr. X's. "I am tired of hearing the same old argument which says that Christ chose only men to be his apostles, and if the apostles had approved of women for ordination, they would have ordained them."

"You must admit that it is a powerful argument."

"I am not so sure about that, Father."

"Why not?"

"I have been thinking. Are you Jewish and circumcised?"

"What kind of a question is that?"

"If all candidates for ordination would have to resemble the 12 apostles, all would have to be Jewish and circumcised. Fishermen and married men would have the first shot because Jesus chose those first. Father, I hate to tell you, you wouldn't stand a chance."

Fr. X noticed a twinkle in Miss Walsh's eyes but he maintained an authoritarian front by cutting her off: "Now wait a minute! We are talking about women."

"O.K. Traditionalists ignore the fact that at the time of the apostles women played no role in public life. That's why there were no female high priests and scribes. If Jesus had chosen women, people would have declared him nuts, but if Jesus were preaching here today, I bet you that the ratio between men and women priests would be 50 to 50."

"You are a smart woman, Miss Walsh. I might put some water on the mill for you by adding that until the ninth century there is evidence of female deacons and that there is written and epigraphic evidence that in the fourth and fifth centuries women were ordained as priests. In December of 1970 several women were ordained in Czechoslovakia to eliminate the shortage of priests under Communism. To my knowledge, Rome has not declared these ordinations invalid, only illicit."

"I did not know that."

"Personally I think that it is a myth that a person, just because she is female, cannot image Christ in an official capacity. We are all called to image Christ, male or female, married or celibate."

"Why then does Rome not declare it immoral to discriminate against 50% of its members, more than 50% if we consider that more women then men attend church?"

"I think that it is partially psychological. Many bishops, especially the cardinals in Rome, are afraid of any major break from tradition. To have a woman in vestments standing next to them behind the altar or serving under one as an associate pastor is unthinkable in their minds. Even many laypersons would need decades to adjust to it. Just think how long it is taking for many people to receive the consecrated host into their hand at communion time, just a minor change like that. Sad to say, but women ordination at this time would create a schism within the church."

"Yeah, traditionalists think nothing of having the consecrated host on their tongues, but in their hands? God forbid! Did the apostles stick out their tongues at the last supper? The sacrament of the Eucharist is being denied to many people on earth because of the shortage of priests. Women ordination would solve that problem."

"No doubt about that. If the successors of Pope John XXIII will be anything like him, we might have optional celibacy and women deacons by the year 2000, but no more than that. Just one more thing: Not every man has a right to ordination. You have to be called by God and the church. The problem is: How do we know who is called? Maybe God is calling women and the church is just deaf."

"Fr. X., you say that too loud and you are going to be silenced. The church is no democracy."

Fr. X laughed at that. "In other words, don't raise your hopes too high. Consider other options to work for the church."

"I feel the calling to be a deacon, and it is not going away."

"Why not teach religion or head a scripture study group? Go for an M.A. and head a CCD program. Consider the Graduate Theological Union in Berkeley for an M.A. I would write you a strong recommendation. Furthermore, have you eliminated the possibility of joining a religious order?"

"No, I have not, but even as a nun I would still be upset about the segregation in our church. We used to have racial segregation in most churches. We got rid of that. Some day we'll have a black pope, ... some day, and long, long, long after that we might have a female pope. By the way, I have met Dominican sisters who share my viewpoint on women ordination. They might accept me into their community."

"Then go for it!"

"Fr. X., I very much appreciate the time you have given me and your openness."

"Any time, Miss Walsh. I hope that we can stay in touch after graduation."

"You bet. In the meantime, have fun grading papers!"

"Thanks a lot, young lady."

A few minutes after Deborah had left she returned and said: "One more argument: Joan of Arc was burned at the stake for being a liberated woman and because she was considered a heretic. Today we venerate her as a saint."

Before Fr. X. could formulate an answer, Deborah was gone, but he mumbled: "Right again."

★★★

It was a quiet evening and Deborah had been sitting for a long time on the front porch gazing at the oak tree and the sunset and mulling over her conversation with Fr. X. Final exams had gone well and graduation was only a few days away. Noticing that his daughter was by herself, Fred came out with a pitcher of ice tea, lemon slices, and sugar.

"A penny for your thoughts, Debbie. You have been sitting here for a long time."

"I am attempting to make a tough decision."

"Oh?"

"I need to decide what to do with my life, not just anything but something fulfilling. This morning I applied for admission to the Graduate Theological Union in Berkeley. Fr. X. helped me with the application and promised a strong recommendation. Remember, some time ago I attended a seminar at that school."

"What kind of a school is it?"

"It was founded or incorporated in 1962. It is interdenominational and offers graduate programs in theology, including Catholic theology. I mailed the application this morning, and with my GPA I am confident that I will get accepted."

"So what's the problem? Is it the tuition?"

"Of course, tuition is the problem. I'll need a scholarship again and, as you know, scholarships hardly ever cover the entire cost. I cannot take any more money from you. That probably means more student loans. What if I run up a high loan balance, get my M.A., and nobody hires me?"

"Are there other options?"

"Two. In 1968 the Vatican approved of married men to become deacons. In San Francisco and Oakland they are already preparing them."

"How does that fit in with you?"

"Well, today they admit married men. Tomorrow they might admit women.

"Debbie, you are a dreamer. You are gambling with your future. They will never ordain women."

"Never say never! In the 15th century, church authorities tacitly consented to it that Joan of Arc should be burned as a heretic and as a much too liberated woman. Four and one half centuries later she was declared a saint."

"Aha, four and a half centuries later. How long do you expect to live? The clergy is macho, especially the Vatican. They don't want women slipping into their ranks. They know it too well from their own mothers and sisters. Women take over. At least, that is what they fear."

"I am talking about deacons, dad. It's not as if I were aspiring to become a bishop."

"If tomorrow you have female deacons, then the day after tomorrow you'll hear the cry for female priests, and that leads to the demand for female bishops. The argument that Jesus chose only men to be his apostles is just a front to cover up a psychological problem. What is your second option?"

"To join a religious order."

"Now that is more realistic. Those nuns do an awful lot of good. Any particular order?"

"I like both the Franciscans and the Dominicans. The Dominicans run schools. I like that, but whether they would want someone like me to face a class of youngsters is questionable. Schools also have other academic jobs like running the library or writing articles for their publications."

"Now we are getting places."

"The Franciscans run hospitals and nursing homes and do social work. I could counsel ill and dying people and their families. Nowadays there are even nuns who work for women's rights and women's ordination. How about that?"

"Debbie, Debbie. You never give up, do you?"

"Never."

"You wouldn't mind if I discussed that with Mom, or would you rather break the news to her yourself?"

"I haven't made a decision, Dad. I am still wrestling."

"Don't wrestle forever. Life is short. I like option # 2. Go for it! I'd better go now. I need to check out the hives for those darn Varroa mites. Mites can destroy a hive in one summer. Thanks for sharing your worries with me."

"Thanks for the tea, Dad. Don't bring those mites into the house."

Deborah stayed on the porch for a long time rubbing her forehead and thinking: *I have nothing to lose by applying for the deaconate. Come to think of it, if no women apply, nothing will ever change. Fr. X. can get me the addresses in Northern California.* "God, make me strong like that beech tree!"

MÉLISSA

Looking back, I am so glad we are not human. God and nature have been good to us for sparing us sleepless nights over what career to follow. I pity them. All we need to be happy is a box or a hollow tree, water, nectar and pollen. Yes, there is anxiety when storms blow or when downpours surprise us while flying from blossom to blossom, or when thieves steal our honeycombs, but humans have that, too. They worry themselves to death. We have each other and forget. Our strength lies in numbers and support. We are all equal. Poor humans!

DEBORAH'S GRADUATION

As had been customary over the years, in 1972 the two graduations at Santa Clara were held in the Mission Gardens, one for the professional graduate schools and one for the undergraduate colleges. It was a most pleasant Saturday in June of that year with the thermometer indicating 85 degrees. In that part of the world one could be 98% certain that there would be no rain.

Fred, Mary, Ruth and Angie occupied four of the chairs on the lawn while Eric preferred to climb one of the historical olive trees to gain a better view. For him the 29-minute wait for the ceremonies seemed endless. The number of police officers and security guards had doubled for this day because of the frequent anti-war protests concerning Vietnam, which always flared up at occasions like graduations.

On Alviso Street, the graduating students, dressed in cap and gown, were getting antsy and fidgety, almost reverting back to their elementary school days. Deborah's face, however, shaded by the cap, revealed both contentment and pride at the culmination of accomplishments at the age of 29. Fred and Mary had bought her the cap and gown with the scarlet colored hood, which identified her as a graduate in Theology.

Finally the band started the graduation march and the Vice Presidents, Deans, and Faculty processed through the center aisle while flashes from cameras flickered all around them. Suddenly the procession came to a halt. Four protestors had prostrated themselves in front of the ROTC cadets, forcing them to step over the protestors. On the following day, one of the local newspapers called it a peaceful demonstration, but a photo showed one of the ROTC cadets accidentally stepping on one of the demonstrators, which the journalist interpreted as the "callousness of the U.S. army." It turned out later that these protestors had been outsiders who moved around from campus to campus.

The procession moved on. After a well-rehearsed address by the President and the conferral of an honorary doctorate, the graduates were called up by their respective Deans for the conferral of the degrees and the congratulatory handshake by the President. Even though the graduating students had been told to hold their applause until their group was done, the cheering for certain classmates sounded like the undisciplined cheering during a ballgame. As soon as the loudspeaker called out "Deborah Walsh, summa cum laude," it sounded like the entire back section of the audience was cheering, but then it resembled cries and wild commotion. Some protestors had turned on part of the sprinkler system with some sprinklers covering a radius of 20 feet. In their confusion it took the security guards two whole minutes to find the turn-off valve. One woman could be heard yelling: "I hope they catch those punks. They should get the death penalty!" The culprits remained unidentified until the Fall quarter when two students began to brag about their heroic deed at a Friday night beer party.

The President apologized and the ceremony went on. Deborah seemed to be in a different world, hardly noticing the commotion. Eric, who had watched the circus from his olive tree, stated during the evening of the graduation party at his grandparents' house that some day, he, too, wanted to attend Santa Clara because graduation had been so much fun. Laughing at his sister who had gotten dripping wet, however, earned him house arrest for the next day, Sunday.

★★★

Less than a week later, Deborah was wandering through the university buildings, no longer as a student but as an alumna. It was a feeling of accomplishment as she strolled through the library, one of the science labs, and the humanities building. A visit to the university would have been incomplete without paying Fr. X. a visit. As usual, he was in his office. All the other faculty offices were dark. *He is going to die here some day*, she thought.

"Good afternoon, Miss Walsh. Have you recuperated from the graduation?"

"What a riot that was!"

"A few years ago I would never have imagined something like that, but Stanford and Berkeley have had worse things happen."

"Father, I don't want to take up much of your time. I am sure that you would like to get out of here and attend to your roses in the Mission Gardens. They are so well taken care of. I have just one question today: Last Saturday I was invited by friends of the family to go to the synagogue with them. They are practicing Jews who, of course, do not believe in the divinity of Christ. They think that we believe in three gods. How can I make them understand that three persons in one God does not imply three gods?"

"Well, Miss Walsh, we are dealing with a mystery which no human being can fully understand and which, for that reason, requires faith. We grew up with the teaching that there are three divine persons in one God and, therefore, have always taken it for granted. Had we not been raised with it, we too might find it irrational. If our human mind could fully understand divine mysteries, and many other Christian teachings, we would elevate ourselves intellectually to the level of God, and that would destroy the mere concept of God as the Supreme Being."

"That ain't helping me in my discussions with them."

"No, it doesn't. But there is an explanation you could use as a first step toward acceptance of the mystery. It would bring them closer to it. Tell them that we, too, believe in only one God. However, in as far as God created everything and in as far as He keeps everything in existence and deeply cares about us, we call Him God the Father. In as far as He became visible on earth in form of a man and lived with us like a human, we call Him God the Son. Had He chosen to be born female, we would call Her God the Daughter. In as far as He enlightens, inspires and motivates us, we call Him God the Holy Spirit. These three manifestations are so pronounced and distinct that we refer to them as persons. That is not entirely orthodox but it is something which they may be able to accept. Once they do, you can go a step further and say that we don't just *refer* to the three manifestations as persons, they *are* three persons in only one God. But that last step will have to wait a while because that is where faith comes in, and we cannot convey faith, only God can.

"Three manifestations of the same God, not bad," Deborah muttered.

"You could also use the picture of a clover leaf. It has three leaves to it but is only one. You have to keep in mind that because of our humanness and our physical bodies, we have no choice but to use terms which we can comprehend, terms like clover leaf, father, mother, son, daughter, persons. God being neither male nor female is as much mother as He is father. We have no other terms. Our minds are limited by what they can visualize. Our brain cells are doing us in."

"I think that I can use some of that the next time it comes up. Thanks for the hints."

"By the way, Miss Walsh, have you come closer to a decision about your future?"

"I still feel drawn to the ministry, to ordination."

"As much as I would like to see it happen, I must tell you that this won't come to pass for many more years. Realistically, you have no choice but to think of another career."

"I know that, Father. That's why I don't sleep as well as I used to."

"Miss Walsh, I believe in the power of prayer. Pray over it, and I promise you that I'll do the same."

"Thank you, Father. See you soon."

"I am looking forward to it, Miss Walsh."

ISABEL

"What is the matter, Isabel? Don't you like this spot for a picnic?"

"Travis, in a way I do. On a muggy day like this one it is nice in the shade of this ancient beech tree and the view of the valley from up here is really something. But this place reminds me too much of her. Didn't I tell you that she comes up here to talk to this tree?"

"You are full of baloney."

"It is true. I saw it."

"I know that she and Ruth have been coming up here since the age of seven, and so have my in-laws."

"Lord, they must all be one of a kind. Some family you married into!"

"You are also one of a kind, a different kind."

"Some gut feeling is telling me that you are working your way back into your family."

"I don't want to talk about it now. Let's enjoy our lunch. I made ham and turkey sandwiches. We also have chips, celery sticks, carrots and for dessert fresh strawberries. For your psychological welfare I brought a bottle of Hearty Burgundy. All healthy stuff."

"Travis, you aren't such a bad chap after all. Is this today's paper?"

"It is."

"Travis, Travis!"

"What?"

"Did you see this? They had graduation at the University of Santa Clara and that scarecrow graduated *summa cum laude,* whatever that means."

"That means that she was in the upper 5% of her class."

"It says here that protesters turned on the water sprinklers during commencement in the mission gardens."

"You must be kidding!"

"Here. Read it for yourself."

"I'll be darned. At Stanford not too long ago they threw a bomb into the Bank of America building. That bank is the symbol of the establishment. In Berkeley they are creating a park in the honor of Ho Chi Minh. Having served in the Air Force in Korea, I cannot condone this type of behavior. They should shoot them all, damn traitors! ... Here, why aren't you eating?"

"I am so jealous! She received scholarships and now she has her B.A. What did I get? San Jose State gave me no scholarship. After one year I had to quit because I could not come up with the tuition."

"You had a low G.P.A., hers was high. During high school you were allergic to books and you spent too much time dancing. She was a bookworm. But that's just as well. Had it been different I might never have met you."

"She would not have been given any scholarships if she looked normal. It's called *reverse discrimination*. It's the same with minorities today. In some colleges they are now the privileged ones."

"That would apply to you, too."

"I would not want any subsidies if they were based on race or nationality."

"And yet, you used the name Sánchez when applying for admission. Isabel, one is beginning to read about reverse discrimination in the papers these days, but how would you feel if you had a physical disfigurement and nobody hired you? Wasn't it nice of the school to give her a lift?"

"I suppose so. … I can already see her walking by me with a condescending look on her face."

"You have a completely distorted image of her. She is one of the kindest persons I ever met."

Isabel's cheeks were twitching. "Have you forgotten the letter she wrote to you?"

"Let's forget that damn letter and enjoy our picnic."

"Okay. … What did you put in here? You know I don't like mayonnaise in ham sandwiches. Give me a slice of Swiss cheese but not that stuff."

"I did not know, honestly." If Isabel had looked at Travis the way she looked at the ham, lettuce and mayonnaise between the bread slices, she would have noticed that she hurt his feelings.

"Come on, you bozo," she said instead. "Pour me a glass of wine and give me one of your cigarettes."

After a while they did eat their lunch, just talking about trivialities. Travis felt that a rift had developed between Isabel and him, and Isabel had been sensing it all along.

★★★

A new movie, *The Exorcist*, was playing, and Isabel wanted to see it. The movie theater smelled of popcorn and sweat. The previews had already started when Isabel said to Travis: "Let's move to an empty row farther back."

"Why? You always wanted to sit in about the tenth row."

She whispered emphatically into his ear: "I don't want to sit next to no popcorn munching nigger for two hours."

"Why don't we just trade seats? He doesn't bother me none," answered Travis, but Isabel was already walking up the aisle. No sooner had they settled down in row 25, than a black family of five chose row 26. One of the boys opened a pop can, which he might have shaken too much, and Isabel felt a mild spray on her neck.

"That does it. I am out of here," she said, left the theatre and Travis had no choice but to run after her. He tried in vain to make her reconsider. They decided to sit on one of those benches under the palm trees between the theatre and the parking lot. Isabel dug through her purse. "Damn, no cigarettes."

"Here, try one of my Camels." Travis lit a match and Isabel inhaled as if to make sure that the most southern tips of her lungs received plenty of the relaxing nicotine. It did calm her down.

After a few minutes Travis broke the silence: "What has been the matter with you lately? Every little mishap irritates you. You know that he did not do it intentionally. Kids are kids."

"He was clumsy," hissed Isabel, and his dad should have pulled his ears and they should have apologized. Just feel my neck. It is sticky from the coke. I was raised in Havana and in New Orleans. There we had an orderly and well-structured society, whites here and colored folks there. No colored boy would have squirted coke onto someone else's neck."

"Isabel, are you deaf? He did not do it intentionally. It seemed to be a very nice family."

"Let's forget it. It is much nicer out here under these palm trees. Let me have another one of those Camels. They are good. Did you know that your sister-in-law does not even know how to smoke a cigarette? A few days ago I saw her at the diner. Everybody at the table smoked and they offered her one, but she barely filled her mouth and blew out the smoke. So I surprised her by walking over to their table and I said to her: 'Debbie, *inhale, … speak, …exhale.'* Unfortunately she would not do it because she knew what would happen. 'Just keep on trying. You'll get the hang of it,' I told her in a nice way. Everybody at the table gave me the dirtiest look you can imagine."

"A look you well deserved. Why are you always so mean to her? If I had been her I would have spat in your face."

"Because she hates me and she wishes that I had never come to California."

Travis noticed that her anger about the careless kid had subsided a little because she could not help laughing about that comment. He said: "Listen, we paid for the tickets. Let's go back in and sit in the last row." It took some fast-talking to be let back in at that point. After 20 minutes or so of watching *The Exorcist*, Travis noticed that Isabel was breathing rather heavily. The throwing up of the possessed girl must have caused that, Travis thought.

"Lack of oxygen and stuffy air," said Isabel. "I need to get some fresh air."

As they walked back to the benches under the palm trees, she went into an uncontrollable coughing spell, and the facial tissue she used to catch her phlegm was reddish with blood. Her chest hurt as she stooped down to cough some more.

"I am taking you to the emergency room at the hospital," Travis said.

"No, you are not. It's nothing. All I need is a drink. Take me to the boarding house. Remember, my grandmother in Havana smoked cigars, coughed all the time, and got to be 92 years old."

"Okay, let's drive to the boarding house," said Travis, but, once in the car, he pushed the button for the flashing lights and stepped on the accelerator. "This time I am not listening to you. We are driving to the hospital."

"All I need is a drink. Take me to the boarding house," she yelled and went into another coughing spell and colored another facial tissue red. "You have no right to take me against my will. I could sue you for that."

"You go right ahead and sue me. It's time for me to get a car phone. Now I could use one."

At the emergency entrance there just happened to be an orderly standing next to a wheel chair taking a smoking break. Travis ran to him and had him bring the wheel chair to the car. It took the two of them to make Isabel sit in it, and within a minute the three had disappeared behind the automatic glass doors.

MÉLISSA

How strange, we all got along so well while harvesting in the fruit trees, bees from different colonies and different races. Italian bees and German bees, bumble bees and mining bees, leafcutter bees and carpenter bees, mason bees and cuckoo bees, we all shared in the resources. If, on the other hand, a bee of a different sort tried to enter our hive, we killed her if she refused to leave.

Why? Why could we not get along as we did in the apple trees? I remember once making room for a bumblebee on the tip of a branch loaded with blossoms because she seemed to be so hungry. We loved those furry bumblebees, but only as long as they did not dare to enter our hive, even on a cold and stormy night. That, however, is so sad.

TRAVIS

"Hi Travis. You are coming here just at the right time to help us with this wheel. It's a flat tire. What's new with you two?" Ruth sounded curious.

"That's why I came to see you. Isabel has been in the hospital for almost a week."

"Car accident? Drunk driving?"

"No, much worse. She was coughing blood. I rushed her to the emergency entrance. X-rays of her lungs show terminal cancer. They give her three to six months."

"How is she taking it?"

"Not too well. She is not a person of faith."

"Does not surprise me."

"There is a black doctor who had been assigned to her case. He is a cancer specialist and thinks that with chemotherapy her life could be extended by another year or two, but Isabel does not want his black fingers to touch her."

Ruth shook her finger at Travis: "And she is the one who spread the rumor about Debbie being a racist. I hope that the doctor stays on her case."

"No, he no longer wants to. Can't blame him. Now she has a young and rather inexperienced intern assigned to her. The hospital won't keep her much longer because her insurance pays hospital rates only for as long as there is hope for recovery. Two weeks ago we rented two rooms at a boarding house. She can stay there until she needs to be in a nursing home. She will have to drag an oxygen tank around with her. Right now she is still feisty."

"In other words, you are going to stay with her."

"Our relationship is shaky. That's why I rented two rooms, but I cannot leave her now in this condition. I once promised her a rosy future in Las Vegas. That's why she gave up her job at the Starlight."

"Well, yes, she needs someone now. Doesn't she have any relatives?"

"She has a no-good brother who is an unemployed drug addict, and her parents are dead."

"In that case, you can't very well leave her now, I fully understand, but you had no qualms about leaving us."

"That's another reason why I came to see you. Having lost her as the principal dancer, I have decided to dump my plan of building up a new nightclub and, consequently, no longer have a need for the $4,000. I have to go back though and undo the arrangements which I have made in Las Vegas. If I cannot find a job up here, how about if I looked for a job down there? I like it in Vegas and you would, too. I know."

"And I know that I would not like raising our kids between casinos. You better find a job up here quickly, because on my wages I cannot support you and the children, especially if you keep on spending money on cigarettes and alcohol."

"No more cigarettes, Ruth, if that will make you happy. Isabel has given me the final push. The day I finish this last pack, I'll quit cold turkey."

"If you are serious about it, quit now, not tomorrow or after the weekend."

"I only have a few left. I won't buy any new ones."

"Come on. Hand them over."

Ruth was astounded that he actually handed them over to her, but he could hardly trust his ears when he heard her flush the toilet of the half bath which one could enter from the garage where the car with the flat tire was. Reemerging, her womanly intuition told her that she had hurt his feelings and she put her arm around him and said: "Come, Travis, let's have a cup of coffee and a piece of coffee cake. The kids should be back any minute. You and Eric can exchange the wheel later. He will be so proud if he can help you with that. Do you like streusel?"

Not looking at her, Travis answered: "Yes, very much." After finishing coffee and cake in silence, on the mantle piece Travis spotted his shoebox in which he had stored his new winter shoes. "What are my shoes doing up there?" he asked.

"Your new winter shoes are in the bedroom closet. Angie needed a box in which to store all of the letters, which she has been receiving. She has gone nuts writing to every Tom and Mary Dickens. She must have 20 steady pen pals by now, two of them in England and one in Australia."

"So that is why she started to write to me every week. We ought to suggest to her to start a stamp collection."

"Yes, she has been receiving some nice commemorative stamps and very nice letters, … from most people that is."

"I was busy."

"Yes, you were always busy, too busy to write a few lines to us. You were even too busy to look for a better paying job while you were still here. It had to be a white-collar job. My dad had to start from scratch when we were little. While working at a cannery, he had a nasty dictator for a boss, but he stuck it out, and he managed to buy a decent- sized house and raise bees on the side. You had a fine job, but after you got laid off, you chose the wrong kind of work. I wish I could put a match to that night club!"

"Thanks Ruth, for once again comparing me to your dad. I don't think that I ever compared you to my mother."

Now she noticed that she had really hurt his feelings and said: "I'm sorry, Travis. I didn't mean to hurt you. I just had to get it out of my system once more. I won't mention it again. I promise."

Before finishing his coffee and without saying a word, he went back to the garage and got busy fixing the tire.

★★★

What a bitch she was this afternoon! But if that's what it takes, then no more cigarettes. I am not so sure I can do it. I wish I had one right now, just one. She could have let me keep those three last ones. What nerve, flushing them down the toilet! Before leaving for Las Vegas, in fact all through our marriage, I had gotten sick and tired of hearing how much more successful her dad was. It didn't do much for my ego or self esteem. It created a feeling of jealousy and failure. Was it my fault that I didn't get hired into better paying jobs?

The kids seemed to be glad to see me. They always do. Eric helped me. Then we finished the streusel. Ruth was right about Eric. I overheard him bragging to Angie that he now knows how to change tires, that he could do it by himself. How will I explain to them that I have to stay a while longer with Isabel? I cannot abandon her after all the promises I made to her, after making love to her. God forbid, should she blabber and my family find out! I have to make sure that they stay away from her.

Making rash promises has always been one of my weaknesses. My parents used to say so. Ruth said it more than once, of course. Isn't everybody entitled to a few faults? Ruth has her faults, too. But then, she did not run away from me. I need a job if I want reconciliation, and I need it fast. Why is Ruth so stubborn about Las Vegas? Of course, with the new electronic industries popping up around here, I cannot argue the fact that jobs will be popping up here as well, but I love Las Vegas. How can I tell Isabel about reconciliation with Ruth? She'll throw a temper tantrum or she'll just cry herself to death, and that would be worse. There is no need for her to know. If only the Walshes could learn to keep their mouths shut!

The next morning Ruth visited her mother.

"Ruth, what's the latest with Travis? Is he going back to Las Vegas with that dancer?"

"No, he has come by the house several times lately, always when the children are in school. Each time it sounds like he is coming around a little bit more in realizing how wrong he was. Yesterday he told me that he has given up on the idea of starting a night club in Las Vegas."

"Oh? I wonder how Isabel is going to react to that. Has he told her?"

"He doesn't have to tell her. She is at Kaiser Hospital with terminal lung cancer. They are giving her three to six months. The few times that I had a chance to talk to her lately I noticed that she was breathing heavily like someone who needs oxygen. Travis caught her coughing and spitting blood. She smoked until she was wheeled into the hospital."

"Ruth, you ought to tell dad. I have been after him for two years now to donate his fancy ivory pipes to a museum, but he won't listen to me anymore. That man is agreeable to everything else, but take his pipe away and he becomes unbearable."

"Pipes are not as bad as cigarettes because you get a lot less smoke into your lungs. You don't intentionally inhale."

"I am not so sure about that. He, too, has been coughing lately."

"Well, Travis promised that he would quit now. I made him give me the ones he still had in his pocket and I flushed them down the toilet. I could tell that I had hurt his feelings but he did not get mad."

"I would take that as a sign that he might want to come back to you."

"Over coffee and cake we had a little bit of an unpleasant exchange, but he went to the garage to fix a flat tire. At that time Angie and Eric came home from school and Eric helped him with the tire. Angie and Eric were happy to see him, and later I overheard a conversation between the two that sounded like all had been decided, dad was coming back. I had the feeling that he would if I asked him to, but not until Isabel is in a nursing home or gone."

"Now wait a minute. If I were you I would tell him, 'either she or we.'"

"That sounds logical, but put yourself into his shoes for a moment. Wouldn't you feel that you had an obligation to her after all this time with her? He lured her from her job, and I am as certain as you are sitting here that he made love to her."

"After what she did to Debbie she deserves no consideration, cancer or no cancer."

"That is looking at it from our side."

"Why can't she be in the boarding house by herself? I bet you he is paying for her room and board."

"But Mom, she is dying. She only has a few months left. After the hospital stay she will probably have to be moved to a nursing home."

"I don't care if it is only for a week. It is the principle."

"Then try putting yourself into her shoes. Your friend lures you away from your job. He promises to marry you and take care of you, and when you are diagnosed with cancer he abandons you."

"She had it coming."

Ruth had to go to the diner now. Friday evenings were always busy times. On the way she deliberated: *Travis is staying with the children until I get back from the diner. What am I going to do? On the one hand I would like to have him back now, but on the other hand he does have an obligation to her. What would the children think if he spent half of the evenings and weekends with us and the other half with her? I don't even want to think about it.*

I also have to break the news to Ernie. Even though there is no real intimacy between us, I can tell that his hopes are high. Is it a sin to wish that she died soon? It would be so much nicer and less nerve wracking if they had stayed in Las Vegas.

ERNIE

The traffic section of the newspaper ran a story entitled: *Second automobile accident on the El Camino Real this week.* It read:

> Last Friday night three automobiles collided as a northbound drunk driver in an Oldsmobile exited at a very high speed from the Laurence Expressway onto the El Camino Real. Witnesses stated that the driver missed the red light and that he plunged his Oldsmobile into a pickup truck eastbound on the El Camino pushing it across three lanes into a cement truck. The driver of the Oldsmobile was pronounced dead by paramedics. His name is being withheld pending notification of kin. The driver of the pickup truck, Ernest Miller, a wallpaper hanger by profession, was taken to Kaiser Hospital. He is in very critical condition with injuries to his head and his chest. The cement truck got away with just a few scratches.

★★★

The hospital looked sparkling clean.

"Ruth, is that you holding my hand?

"No, Ernie, this is Deborah. How are you feeling?"

"Hugh?"

"How are you feeling?"

"I have felt better. I can hardly breathe. My chest hurts. Tell the nurse to give me more morphine, please."

"Ernie, I'm sorry. The doctor said that more morphine could kill you."

"I'm going to die anyway. I can feel it. I may not be the smartest, but they cannot fool me." Ernie sounded so weak that Deborah could hardly hear him. His head was wrapped up in bandages with only his nose, mouth, and ears showing.

"Ruth is coming as soon as she gets off work."

"Tell her to bring me some of her coffee. It might help me to sit up. My ears are cold."

"Okay Ernie, I'll call her. You need to rest now, Ernie. I'll cover your ears."

"One more thing, Deborah. Would you tell my mom to give Chip the $200 I owe him? She can take it out of my savings account."

"I sure will."

"Hold my hand. I am afraid. I am afraid of dying."

"Oh, Ernie. You have always been such a good man. No need to be afraid. When the time comes for you to die, you will go straight to heaven."

"How can you be sure?"

"I know it. Trust me. ... You need to sleep now, Ernie."

"Just one more thing: How long have I been here?" His voice had gotten so faint that Deborah had to bend down all the way to understand him.

"Five days, Ernie."

"What happened to my car?"

"Your car is in worse shape than you are. You got hit by a drunk driver."

"Who was the other driver?"

"Don't know. All we know is that he was drunk and ran a red light."

"Always the alcohol! ...God have mercy on him. ... Will God have mercy on me? I can't even remember when the last time was I confessed my sins. I'm afraid."

If I could be a priest now, thought Deborah. *What a blessing that would be!* She bent down all the way to his ears and said: "Listen, Ernie. The minute you tell God that you are truly sorry for your sins, your sins are forgiven."

"Sure?"

"Absolutely sure, but I promise you, I'll call a priest."

"What does heaven look like?"

"Ernie, no eye has ever seen and no ear has ever heard what God has prepared for those who love him." Deborah wanted to say a few prayers with him but his eyes had closed and he was falling asleep. Deborah kept holding his hand until she had finished wording a prayer for him anyway. By that time he was sound asleep. Although he was breathing quite heavily, he seemed to be at peace.

★★★

Thick raindrops were splashing against the windows of the hospital. After briefly talking to the nurse at the nurses' station, Ruth came down the hallway and ran into Deborah. "Debbie, how is he?" she asked with a trembling voice.

"Very weak. He talked a lot but I had a difficult time making out what he was saying. His hearing is very good. He believes that he is dying. His chest was hurting him but now he has dozed off. He asked for more morphine but his doctor thinks that it would be too risky to give him more."

"I hope that it is not too late to tell you this: Please, do not let him know that Travis has moved back in with us. We are giving our marriage another try. It would kill him."

"I think you got that right. It would kill him."

"Debbie, I love him dearly and he has a crush on me, but there is no way that I could spend the rest of my life with him. He is so unbelievably timid and indecisive, complicated and jittery. It amazes me that he drives as well as he does."

"Ruth, there is no need to rationalize about this any further. His mother told me today that the doctors are giving him no more than a week. I'll be back to pray with him. His mom and dad are coming back after supper. They know the details."

"If he is in pain and has only a week, then why the hell does the doctor withhold the morphine?"

"I don't know. By the way, Ernie asked me if you could bring him some of your coffee."

"He did? I can't go home just for that. I'll get some in the cafeteria downstairs. At this juncture he can no longer distinguish between good and average coffee."

"And if he asks whether you made it yourself, which I am sure he will, you have to tell him a lie because the only thing that matters to him is that you made it and that you give it to him. So, run home and make some. Right now he is asleep anyway."

"I cannot lie to him, but if Travis sees me leave with the coffee, … Lord, what a mess have I gotten myself into!"

"Here, take my umbrella. You'll need it. Ernie wants me to call a priest. I'll do that right now.

The wind made a hollow sound around the windows as Deborah accompanied her sister to the lobby. By the time she got back to the second floor to have the nurse call a priest, she saw a nurses aide standing in Ernie's doorway waving at the head nurse who was trying to catch up with her paper work. Deborah was asked not to come into Mr. Miller's room for now, and when after ten minutes the nurses emerged, the head nurse asked Deborah if she was a relative of Mr. Miller.

"No, but a close friend," she answered.

The nurse cleared her throat and said: "We are so sorry. He passed away in his sleep. We'll call his parents and his doctor."

Deborah limped to the phone as fast as she could and called Travis to let Ruth know as soon as she got home. Then she went to Ernie's room. The little that could be seen of his face and his hands appeared to be as peaceful as they did when she left him 30 minutes ago. After stroking his hair, she went to the window to say a prayer for him and his parents. The bed next to the window was empty allowing her to gaze at the park-like landscaping. "Lord, if there ever was an innocent man, it was Ernie. Please, grant him your beatific vision and let his family find consolation."

The rain had stopped and the winds were moving the clouds westward. The raindrops on the crab apple trees on the side lawn glistened like gold in the evening sun, which was quietly reemerging. A lonesome bumblebee had survived the storm and was about to fly home, probably empty handed, but nevertheless, home.

UPHILL BATTLE

Edith was moving out of the freshmen dorm and she hoped that for the Fall Quarter she could check into the Campisi residence center which was known to be less noisy. Deborah helped her pack. After the station wagon of Edith's parents had been stuffed, the two decided to relax in a quiet corner of a coffee shop nearby for lunch. Edith noticed that Deborah was not her usual self. She lacked the peppiness and cheerfulness she normally displayed when she was with Edith.

"What's going on Debbie? I can tell that something is bothering you."

Even though Edith was eight years Deborah's junior, and though she was not Catholic, Deborah opened up to her by telling her that every diocese in which she had applied for admission to the deaconate program had sent her a negative reply. "I feel rejected," she said. "All of them used the same reply: In the Catholic Church ordination is reserved for men.

"I know that I should not feel so rejected because my parents, my sister, and even Fr. X. had told me that this was going to happen. My dad once said: 'Why waste your time on this? Our church is run by men, some of whom feel threatened by women.' I should have listened."

Deborah pulled out a handkerchief and Edith said: "I know that when it comes to ordination and church government, your church discriminates against more than 50% of its members, because church attendance among women is higher than it is among men, just as it is in our church. In the Methodist Church we have female pastors, not many, but the door is open. It's a new movement. You ought to join us because this issue seems to be shortening your life."

"Don't tempt me," said Deborah with something that could pass for a smile. The LCA Lutherans also ordain women and the Episcopalians are discussing it."

"For what it is worth, I believe that your application may have achieved more than you think," Edith added after a while. "If nobody ever applies, the attitude of your hierarchy will never change. They need to hear it over and over again because many of them are hard of hearing. If in each diocese dozens of theologically educated women were to follow your example, it would eventually alter the frozen mindset of at least some of your bishops, and some day, some of them might muster the courage to lay the cards on the table during their visits with the pope and those rigid fuddy-duddies around him. What is needed are candid talks, not those genuflecting kissing-his-ring talks. Your letter may already have caused your bishop to do some open minded thinking."

"Girl, where have you learned to talk like that?"

"It goes with the name Daring. In my family we always communicate like that, no sugar coating."

"I doubt that letters like mine even reach the bishop's desk. His staff wants to save him the agony …"

"… and do a great disservice to your church."

"The Vatican has always been very slow in approving any major change. They waste precious time discussing trifles like whether and when to ring the bell during mass and when to genuflect and when to bow. There may be no change in our lifetime, but the problem is that I feel the calling now, not on my death bed."

"Well, what did I tell you? Join us. We all believe in the same Jesus Christ as our savior, the same bible, the same baptism, we all work toward the same goal. I'll introduce you to our pastor. She is a woman. She understands."

"Not so fast, young lady. I have to sleep over this. Yes, we have the same goals and the same basic teaching, but there are also significant differences. Tempting as it sounds, -- and believe me, you are a temptress, -- a decision like that ..."

"I'll pick you up tomorrow morning at 9:00. Don't oversleep. You Catholic women have been sleeping much too long."

"Edith, I know you mean well, but as I wanted to say, a decision like that I need to roll back and forth in my brain. Let's go and have lunch. After that you can drop me off at St. Joseph's Hall. I need to talk to Fr. X. once more."

Driving to the restaurant, Edith grabbed Deborah's hand and said: "No matter what you decide, we will always remain close friends." After a minute they had reached the restaurant and Deborah answered: "That means a lot to me."

★★★

The response from the Graduate Theological Union came sooner than expected. Deborah was sitting on the front porch when she opened the envelope with an ounce of trepidation. The letter read:

Dear Miss Walsh,

I am happy to inform you that the Office of Admissions and the screening committee have approved your application for admission to the graduate program in Catholic Theology. Your academic background and the letters of recommendation are impressive.

At the same time, I am sorry to have to inform you that at this time no financial aid is available. Our budget is stretched to the limit. I hope that in the next fiscal year scholarship money will become available for you.

I am looking forward to meeting you on the day of orientation which is September 1. Once again, congratulations.

Sincerely,

Rev. David Rippon, Ph.D.

Director of Admissions

In spite of the friendly tone of the letter and the words of praise, Deborah felt like crying because there was no way that her family could come up with the money for tuition plus room and board, and considering the uncertainty in her case of ever finding a halfway decently paying job, she felt that adding to the student loan, which she already carried, was far too risky. For the first time since losing her job at the city library she broke into tears. Since her parents were not home, she did not have to hide them, but because their car could pull up the driveway any minute, she decided to go for a long walk and sit down in the cool shade of the beech tree on the hill and, hopefully, come to a decision on what to do now.

The walk to the beech tree was a long stretch uphill and Deborah was glad that she had taken her walking cane that she had never used on campus.

"You are indestructible," she whispered. "Under your majestic branches I have always found strength and new ideas."

Halfway up the hill she was still thinking and talking to herself and the tree, when she heard noises coming from the top of the hill, noises that sounded like those of chain saws. Soon a huge flatbed came laboring up the hill in low gear and passed her up. What she then saw from afar almost made her heart stop. Tree fellers and lumber jacks were felling her beech tree. What was left of it at this point was only its immense trunk stretching out two majestic arms into the blue sky like two black silhouettes wanting to touch heaven. Deborah stood there paralyzed. Little by little she felt a mixture of anger and frustration building up in her, but she realized the futility of arguing with the loggers because they were only doing what they had been told to do, and by now the tree had seen its better days anyway. At this point it looked like a gigantic cross on Golgotha.

She turned around. The walk downhill was more cumbersome for her than climbing the hill. When after a while two of the loggers passed her up in their small Ford pick-up, with windows rolled down, she heard one of them say: "It is going to take all day tomorrow to cut through that ancient trunk. I have never seen a monster like that in my life." That gave Deborah a small feeling of satisfaction. *I hope it will take them a week, and may their chainsaws go dull and break several times!*

A week later she went up there again. The trunk with its powerful arms was still standing. Children had already discovered the opportunity of climbing those branches, which had not yet been removed from the premises. The kids resembled monkeys in a zoo. She recognized two of the boys. They were from the Hilbert family that belonged to the Episcopal Church, and suddenly she thought: *I am going to pay the Episcopal pastor a visit. They are closer to us Catholics than the Methodists. When I saw the liturgy in Edith's church it did not appeal to me.* She felt that the beech tree had done its job once again, -- for the last time.

★★★

Deborah had already shared the letter from the Theological Union with her parents but she had not yet had the courage to mention the possibility of leaving the Catholic Church. She knew that it would hit them like a bomb because they did not fully grasp how strong her desire was to be ordained. She had to wait for the proper moment, and if nothing worked out, there was no need to administer the shock treatment at all. The next day, while her dad was socializing with his bees and her mom had gone shopping, she picked up the phone and called the Rev. John Flynn, pastor of the Episcopal Church. He listened attentively as she explained that she had majored in Catholic theology and told him about her desire to be ordained a deacon. Impressed by her explanation, -- she always verbalized well, -- he invited her to his parsonage by saying: "Isn't it a coincidence that tomorrow afternoon one of the professors from our seminary and his wife are coming to visit, and it happens to be that the professor's wife is an ordained deacon. How about joining us for tea or coffee?

"I would love to," answered Deborah. She sounded hyper.

"Would four in the afternoon suit you, Miss Walsh?"

"Four in the afternoon would be splendid."

"All right, come as you are, informal. I am looking forward to another conversation. I'll tell my wife to set the table for five."

Four in the afternoon. It sounds like a detective story. God, let me be a good detective.

Deborah was overjoyed and called Edith. "Edith, I need a ride tomorrow afternoon. My car is in the repair shop. Can you take me?"

"Where to?"

"To the Episcopal church at the Bay."

"Edith was shrewd and quick. "All right, I'll take you, but under the condition that next Sunday you come to our church once more."

"It's a deal," said Deborah.

The next day Edith dropped her off at the Episcopal parsonage and said: "Call me when you are ready to be picked up."

Suddenly, a strange feeling overcame Deborah. *Is it right to leave my church over just one issue? Would I give up my U.S. citizenship because I disagreed with the president and my governor and their policies? Washington ... Rome ... What's the difference?*

It was around 4:00 p.m. and Mrs. Flynn answered the doorbell. Seeing Deborah, she did not even wait for her to introduce herself but said: "I assume that you would like to talk to the pastor but today is a very busy day. At the moment we have company and we are expecting another person any minute. Would it inconvenience you a lot to come back tomorrow?"

"Oh, my name is Deborah Walsh. Your husband is expecting me for tea at 4:00."

"Mrs. Flynn blushed and said: "I am so sorry. Won't you come in and make yourself comfortable here in the office. I'll tell my husband that you're here." The conversation coming from the living room sounded very lively. Everybody seemed to be talking at the same time like at an Italian gathering. When the pastor entered the office, Deborah could not help noticing a puzzled look on his face but, diplomatic as he was, he shook hands with her and said: "I'm so glad you could make it. Let's join Prof. Shilling and his wife in the living room."

Upon entering the living room, Prof. and Mrs. Shilling stood up and introduced themselves. From the conversation that ensued it became clear that Pastor Flynn had already told the guests the reason for Deborah's visit. Their thorough knowledge about the Catholic Church did not surprise Deborah because Prof. Shilling taught Church History. He also knew that there had been deaconesses in the early church.

"I know where you are coming from," he said. "The ordination of women is altogether new in the Episcopalian and Anglican Churches. Many of our parishioners find it hard to accept women celebrating the Eucharist. Many reject the idea outright, but then there are others, especially the more educated, who emphasize that the church is not going far enough to bring about social justice within the church, and they ask for even more changes. Half of our members, however, are just as conservative as the ones in your church who fear that the Second Vatican Council paved a dangerous path."

Very bluntly, like out of nowhere, the deaconess said: "I sense that you are very progressive in your thinking, but I trust that you are also aware of the special problem which you carry with you. I mean, ... well, have you ever thought of studying parish administration and applying for those very important desk jobs in parish offices? The people who work behind the scenes are just as important as the preachers who wear the vestments and face the congregation."

Deborah understood all too well what the deaconess was saying, but she had not expected that to come from a progressive minded woman, a woman who had been able to fulfill her own dreams. She felt somewhat embarrassed, and before she could think of a proper response, Mrs. Flynn called everyone to the dining room table. The table was set with very expensive china from England. The exquisite cups were translucent so that you could see your fingers through them. Mrs. Flynn served two very delicious-looking coffee cakes, one with streusel and one with a peach topping. After everyone was seated Mrs. Flynn asked Deborah whether she preferred coffee or tea. Deborah chose coffee but everyone else drank tea. *Why couldn't she have asked the others first? I would have chosen tea also.*

The conversation went from comments about the weather to the declining offertory collections on Sundays, and finally to the topic of interfaith communion. They wanted to know what Deborah's viewpoint was on that.

"I have no problem with interfaith communion as long as the recipient believes in the real communion with Christ. Transubstantiation or consubstantiation, I don't care. What difference does it make whether Christ comes to me in the form of bread and wine or with bread and wine, whether I become united with Him in our church or in your church. Or may a church claim Christ for herself and her members only?" Deborah could feel the reservation at her bluntness. They obviously did not believe in interfaith communion.

"The cake is delicious," said the pastor. "Have another piece, Miss Walsh." Deborah was still puzzled by Mrs. Shilling's statement in the living room. She declined the cake but took a refill on the coffee.

Finally the pastor returned to the topic of women's ordination. "You realize, of course, that you would first have to go through the process of joining the Episcopal Church. We would love to have you. Then you would have to apply for admission to the seminary and get accepted."

"I have already been accepted at the Graduate Theological Union in Berkeley," answered Deborah. Their eyes opened wide.

"Congratulations! But that is different from getting accepted for ordination." remarked the deaconess. "Many factors besides academic preparation come into play here."

Prof. Shilling added: "My wife's suggestion to study parish administration and learn the ins and outs in a parish office is not such a bad one. A large parish cannot function without such expertise."

The verdict was in, and Deborah just nodded politely. *Did I graduate "summa cum laude" in Theology to become a pencil pusher?* The coffee cake was very tempting, but when Mrs. Flynn offered Deborah a second piece she politely declined saying that she had to watch her weight. She immediately realized that this was a mistake. She should have accepted. I can be so stupid, she thought. There wasn't much conversation after that and she did not feel like discussing ordination any further that afternoon. Looking at her watch she said: "I'd better call Edith who drove me here to come and pick me up because she needs to be home for supper. They also have company." Mrs. Shilling kindly offered to drive her home and Deborah called Edith to let her know that she had a ride. She thanked Pastor and Mrs. Flynn for the kind invitation, the stimulating conversation and the delicious cake. On her way out in the hallway she overheard the professor say something like: "She is a lot smarter than she appears to be."

On the way home Deborah said to Mrs. Shilling: "You must have felt a strong calling for your vocation."

"Yes, I did, and the calling is still there to go one step further and become an ordained priest or minister, as we prefer to call it, after more theological training, of course."

"Then you would not have felt fulfilled with an office job in a parish office."

"No, that kind of job would not fulfill me. That was not and is not my vocation. I feel that I belong where I am. I love to preach now and then and perform baptisms and weddings."

Deborah made no response and the chilling silence made the deaconess realize how inconsiderate her answer had been. She understood Deborah's silence and wished that she would say something. At her parent's house Deborah thanked Deacon Shilling for the ride and politely asked if she cared to come in for a cup of tea, but Mrs. Shilling declined with the same politeness. Deborah wished her a pleasant evening and that ended the conversation. Mrs. Shilling waited until Deborah had entered the house before she drove off, and then she drove off very slowly.

MÉLISSA

There is one thing I learned when I was still young. Shortly after seeing my distorted face reflected in a drop of water, some of my sisters and brothers avoided me. I felt that I was being ignored at times. I also did not like the location of our beehive. It had been placed too far away from orchards. Other bee colonies had it so much better, I thought. Their hives were in the midst of orange groves. Consequently, I decided to join one of them. To impress them I first loaded up with nectar and pollen. Then I landed on the platform of a hive right under a sweet smelling orange tree. The guard bees sniffed me and let me pass as if inviting me in. I unloaded. *The younger bees took the nectar from me, but in spite of the darkness, I could feel that they looked at me funny. Nevertheless, I felt at home until some of my new sisters sensed that I was from a different colony. Suddenly they jumped on me and showed me the door. I was lucky I barely made it to freedom.* "Girl," *I said to myself after I landed on a branch with sweet aroma,* "don't leave home. The grass always appears greener on the other side of the fence."

THE HEART IS A LONELY HUNTER

Deborah was facing a mirror. *What now? In my own church I will never get ordained. Never? Maybe, when I am 70. My curse is to have been born a girl. The Episcopalians hinted at a different reason as to why I should forget my ambition to stand behind the altar. Try the Lutheran Church? It would be more of the same. Look at me. I cannot change my nose or my chin or my limping and being a little hunched over. Mom tells me how beautiful my hair, my forehead, and my eyes are. She is right, but that won't do the trick. Edith wants me to switch over to the Methodists. I would miss the Eucharist in their liturgy. If I had a lot of money I would undergo plastic surgery. Some smaller church might accept me.*

Ordination would, however, not be the same as in my church because they lack apostolic succession. The whole thing does not feel right. Maybe, just maybe, … there could be a reason why I was born this way. Maybe, God has other plans for me. Could it be that He needs a face like mine? If a person who has everything going for herself tells a person who is down in the dumps, "I know how you feel," *she won't come across as credibly as a person who herself has a burden to carry. The afflicted person might think: Yeah, she has it easy talking. She cannot possibly know how I feel. Could God have made me like this for a reason? My eyes, my forehead, and my hair are pretty. Mom is right, -- but that is all that's pretty. For the rest I am a scarecrow. What now?*

She sat down at her desk to think. Supporting her head in the palm of her right hand, her eyes became fixed on a painting next to her bookcase. It was a reduction of "Christina's World" by Andrew Wyeth dating back to 1948. The painting, as plain and as realistic as it is, acquired a lot of notoriety in art circles. The only reason why Deborah fell in love with this print was that she saw herself in Christina. The painting shows a large grassy hill in a mixture of green and brown with a farmhouse and a small barn on top of the hill. In contrast to the drab color of the hill and the farmhouse, the artist named her Christina, a young, slightly crippled woman, in a white dress, which appears pinkish from the invisible evening sun. She is lying on the grass trying to raise herself up, supported by a slightly deformed arm and cramped hands. So much realism! She raises up her head, and though we cannot see her face, her eyes are fixed on the home on the hill, a home she tries to reach. She seems exhausted and wants to make one last attempt to reach her goal. Behind her thick and dark hair, which is in a slight disarray, one suspects a beautiful and determined face. Deborah could not take her eyes off that painting. *I have always liked that scene. It grabs the inner me and makes my mind wander. Tomorrow I'll go to the public library and check out the book "The Heart is a Lonely Hunter," by Carson McCullers. I don't know if it fits Christina's mood and mine, but the title appeals to me and I have always wanted to read it.*

★★★

Deborah scanned the aisles for *The Heart is a Lonely Hunter*, but walking slightly bent over, she had a hard time looking up at the top shelves. According to the call number the book had to be up there. At that moment her old librarian friend Juanita González happened to be shelving books and saw her.

"Debbie, what a surprise! Haven't seen you in such a long time. I did not know if you were alive or dead."

"Hi, Juanita. Yes, I should have shown my face around here now and then, but I still do not feel very comfortable in this building."

"I understand. What have you been into lately?"

"You know that I graduated from the U. of Santa Clara. I am now trying to decide what to do with my life. I still teach the ABC's to some of my former students who at this point have learned to read the newspaper. I couldn't just leave them in the lurch."

"You never give up."

"Never say 'never'! I had wanted to prepare for the ministry in our church ..." Deborah stopped. *No, I better not go into this now. I know that Juanita is a Pre-Vatican II Catholic. She would not understand ...*

"You are nuts. Any other possibilities?"

"Well, yes. I would like to go to graduate school, but that may be financially out of reach. I wouldn't mind working for some charity organization, but those organizations cannot pay a living wage with benefits. Nursing homes would be a possibility. That would come closer to working in the ministry if I were given the chance to work directly with patients. For that I might have to go into nurses' training first."

"I admire your idealism, Debbie."

"No need to canonize me yet. I was trying to get that fat novel on the top shelf, but I cannot reach up that high."

"*The Heart is a Lonely Hunter.*" Why do you want to read such a depressing book? You need something to cheer you up."

"How do you know it's depressing? Have you read it?"

"No, but doesn't the title tell you enough?"

"The title fits my state of mind right now."

"You ought to come over to our house some time this week. My husband hardly knows you. We'll play some peppy music and have a glass of wine. Could you come Sunday afternoon?"

"I would love to but I cannot promise you for sure. I'll let you know."

After Deborah had checked out the book and left the library, Juanita ran into Mrs. Crawfish. "Hi, Mrs. Crawfish, I just saw Deborah Walsh. She was checking out a book."

"Oh? What is she into now?"

"She is keeping quite busy. I assume that you know that she graduated from the U. of Santa Clara, but she hasn't found a job yet. She still teaches reading and writing to some of her former students who have progressed to reading the newspaper. I am just curious, do you think at this point that terminating her services was the best way to go?"

"Mrs. González, that woman talks to trees, so I heard. Do you consider a person normal who talks to a tree?

"Mrs. Crawfish, we all have our fantasy icons that we treasure, be it a special painting, a sculpture, a musical piece, a photo, a flowering garden, or whatever turns us on."

"But do you talk to them?"

"In my mind I do. Mike Wilkins talks to his Ferrari. We all consider him to be normal."

"You may have a point there." At that Mrs. Crawfish hurried off claiming that she had a very tight schedule this morning.

Before leaving the library, Juanita stopped at the ladies' room. There she saw Deborah facing a mirror. She had not noticed Juanita coming in, and Juanita heard her whispering: "Mirror, mirror, on the wall, who is the fairest of them all. – God, why me? Why me?" – Juanita tiptoed out as quietly as she had come in.

ON THE PORCH

It was a quiet but humid and muggy afternoon when Deborah sat on the porch meditating about the possible directions her life might take. Today she would have liked to climb the hill to visit her favorite beech tree, or what was left of it, but her hips were hurting her as if arthritis had found its way into her joints much too early. If she could not run she would rather sit here and watch the bumblebees in the flowering bushes alongside the porch. They took her back to the hospital on that evening when Ernie died, to that lonely bumblebee who was about to fly home after the rainstorm. *God, grant Ernie his well-deserved glory. He always was so innocent. He has reached his home. What is left for me to do now with my life?*

The doorbell of the front door rang. Deborah limped to the entrance hall and spotted two women at the door. No, not the Jehovah's witnesses again, she thought. They were always so persistent. She had read several editions of the *Watch Tower,* which had been left at the front steps. What bothered her was, while the articles on family values were well written and worth reading, biblical quotes were frequently cited and interpreted out of context, and the writers who predicted the end of time would inevitably read a lot into the bible's symbolic numbers and images that could not be substantiated. She had gotten tired of idealistic evangelists who recited a memorized text without really understanding scripture theology. But the more she disagreed with them the more witnesses had been sent to her by the elders.

I will simply tell them that I am not feeling well today, she thought, and that would not be a lie. Opening the door, however, she noticed immediately that the two young ladies standing there were not Jehovah's witnesses. They seemed to be members of the Church of Jesus Christ of Latter Day Saints, commonly known as Mormons. Mormons had always impressed her with their biblical knowledge and she invited them in, took them to the porch and offered them a cup of coffee. She felt foolish and embarrassed when the two ladies declined the offer and some guilt feeling overcame her. Had she and her family become addicted to that caffeine brew?

"How about a glass of cold lemonade," she asked.

"We would love some," the two answered in unison, and within five minutes Deborah came out with a pitcher of ice-cold lemonade and a small plate with lemon cookies. Anything cold on an afternoon like this one would have to create friendship.

"By the way, I am Sister Deborah and this is Sister Julie. You may call us Debbie and Julie." Sister Deborah had beautiful facial features and gorgeous hair, and Julie looked so much like her sister Ruth, except that she was a brunette. Both seemed to be college age. Deborah had nearly spilled the sugar from her teaspoon when she heard her name. "And I am Deborah Walsh," she said. You may call me Debbie as well. As Debbie Walsh had expected, the conversation turned out to be a pleasant one. She soon felt that the two ladies were no dummies. They knew their theology. Even though they looked at her when they spoke, they never stared. I would fit right in with them, she thought. She enjoyed the ensuing discussion in spite of their differences on topics like apostolic succession of the bishops, the Eucharist, and the ordination of women. The two missionaries did not believe in the real presence of Christ in the consecrated bread and wine. When they felt how down and frustrated Deborah Walsh was over the issue of women ordination, Sister Deborah took her hand.

"Debbie," she said, "it's okay to call you Debbie?"

"Of course, I like it, as I told you."

"Debbie, our church will never ordain women, but that does not upset me at all because I believe that God has special assignments for each one of us which are just as important as those of the clergy."

"I wish I could feel that way. I find it a little hypocritical that a church which preaches social justice excludes 50% of its members from offices in that church."

"Debbie, you have been created for a purpose, and so were Julie and I, and it is not for us to meddle in God's plans for us."

"I never thought of it this way." Debbie looked at Sister Deborah skeptically however, because she thought that God's plans for her and many other women might well be ordination and that her church might simply be deaf to God's voice. However she decided not to argue the point because she was in no mood to argue. Sister Deborah had a tone of voice which made everything she said sound so sincere and even convincing. It made Deborah Walsh refrain from arguing in order not to disturb the feeling of friendship, which she felt developing between the three of them. A moment of silence ensued and Julie asked: "Has it ever occurred to you that God may have had a hand in it when your parents chose the name Deborah for you?"

"How is that?"

"Well, there were two Deborahs in the Old Testament, two very important women, one in the Book of Genesis and later on another one in the Book of Judges. The one in the Book of Judges was originally a homemaker like all women at that time, but then she became a military advisor and a judge. She was greatly respected for her wisdom and eloquence. In fact, together with Barak, who was one of Israel's most capable generals at the time, she worked out a military plan and was believed to be a voice of God. She told Barak: GO! Which meant: Go into battle, and the general answered: 'If you come with me, I'll go. If you do not come with me, I will not go.' (Judges: 4.8). Isn't it unbelievable that at that time, when women's roles were confined to the home, a general would depend on the moral support of a woman? Never, however, would Deborah have been considered for the position of High Priest. That role was reserved for men, and that did not bother her because she had found her calling."

Debbie remarked how impressed she was with Sister Julie's explanation of Scripture, but to herself she thought: How would you know that Judge Deborah did not feel the calling to the role of a High Priest?

Then Sister Deborah began to elaborate on the role of the other Deborah in the Book of Genesis. That lady was just as important but in a different vocation. She was a nurse and the midwife to a variety of women and to Rebekha who was Isaac's wife. She also taught Rebekha how to run a large household, but her fame rested on her medical skills. Have you ever considered the role of a nurse?"

"With my face?" asked Debbie. She actually had a smile from ear to ear.

"Debbie, if I were the patient, what would count is not the face but the soul and the skills of my nurse. Don't let anyone intimidate you. Your words to a suffering person would probably count a lot more than those of a nurse who looks like a Hollywood star with a porcelain doll's face and without a cross to bear."

There was silence. "The thought has crossed my mind also," Debbie said after a while. "We are on the same wavelength. Thanks for reconfirming something in me. But to get back to the Deborahs: What got you so interested in them?"

"It is because of the namesakes that these women caught my interest. I would like to add that in Hebrew the name Deborah signifies a bee. A bee always works for others, for her large family, for her community, and that is what the two Deborahs did."

"A bee!" Deborah repeated out loud. "I have been nicknamed 'honeybee' many times. Did you know that we raise bees?"

"No, we did not know that," answered Sister Deborah. "Bees have always had some mythological significance for me. In ancient Greek they called a honeybee *mélissa*. By the way, I see that you have an oak tree on your front lawn. How appropriate! In the book of Genesis it says that after Rebekha's nurse Deborah died, Deborah was buried below Bethel under an oak tree. That tree was called *Oak of crying*. I believe it's in chapter 5."

"An oak tree?" asked Debbie. It must have been an old and majestic tree that they gave it a name. I have always been fond of majestic trees. I need to read up on those two Deborahs."

"Can we come back some day?" asked Sister Deborah. We enjoyed this visit but we need to be on our way now."

"Any time. It was a pleasure."

The two left and Deborah noticed that they spent a minute beholding the oak tree and the bee hives at a distance. *So I am not the only admirer of trees. I may, however, be the only nut who talks to trees. It is unbelievable, Deborah meaning honeybee. Those two emancipated women in the Bible found their vocation. … Oak of crying. … Dear God, what is my vocation?*

SANTERÍA

Three months after Mary had heard from Ruth of Isabel's fate, she changed her hostile attitude toward Isabel. One day she said to Fred: "Why harbor hatred against someone who is facing death in a nursing home. So what if she is different! We are all different. Ruth tells me that Travis visits her only once a week, and those are the only visits she gets. Poor woman! She must feel deserted. I am going to pay her a visit."

The hallways of the nursing home smelled of a mixture of coffee and disinfectants. A custodian was pushing a vacuum cleaner while whistling the tune of "God bless America." As there was no one at the nurse's station, Mary asked him: "Would you happen to know what room Miss. Macintosh is in?"

"She is just down the hall, room 103. Watch out. She seems to be in a bad mood today."

The door was open. Isabel was hooked up to an oxygen tank.

"Hi Isabel. Remember me?"

"Who are you? … Oh no, not you of all people!"

"Isabel, I came to make peace. How are you feeling?"

"Well, I'll be darned! Did you say peace?"

"Yes, that's what I said, and it comes from the heart."

"There is no peace around here. The minute I doze off hoping for pleasant dreams, they come to wheel me down the hall for my daily bath, and I hate it. I turn on my favorite TV show, and Mrs. Erwin over there begins to complain and scream. She is a little … you know what. I am on the waiting list for a private room. You came just at the right time, because at this hour they normally come for my bath."

"Fred is sending his greetings and a little jar of honey. Travis told Ruth that you prefer honey in your coffee."

"Thanks. At least someone thinks of me. Haven't seen Travis in a while. First he came every day, then every other day, and now I am lucky if I see him once a week."

"I am sure that you know that a month ago he moved back in with his family. They want to give marriage another try." Mary could not help it that deep down she was experiencing some spiteful satisfaction breaking the news to Isabel while at the same time feeling guilty about it. -- *Hadn't I come to be nice to her?* -- Isabel turned red in her face, sat up in bed and yelled: "What? That backstabbing, fucking liar! No wonder he shies away from me. He promised me a great future in Las Vegas."

Isabel had tears in her eyes. She pulled the tube away from her nose and soon began gasping for air. Mary was just about to run for a nurse when an orderly came with a wheel chair.

"Miss Macintosh, it is time for your bath."

"Drop dead, man," she yelled."

Being familiar with her antics, he paid no attention to her. He grabbed her by the arm to help her into the wheel chair.

Mary intervened: "Sir, she is in no condition right now to take a bath."

"Thanks, Mary," Isabel said, but because the orderly was still holding her by the arm, she spitefully looked at his face and said: "Get your black hands off me."

The orderly gave up, went down the hall to the bathroom facilities to ask the attending women to get her. Being Afro-American, one of them said: "Let's skip the damn bath today. I have had just about enough of her insults." The orderly went back to Isabel's room and simply said: "No bath today."

He is good looking, thought Mary. *Seems to be a man with a lot of patience.*

"Isabel, that man is only doing his job. That was not a nice thing you said to him."

"I am for strict segregation. Why can't we have two sets of nursing homes."

"When you still had strict segregation In New Orleans, white nursing homes hired black cooks, janitors, and aides, and white families hired black nannies."

"Okay, you are right. I am a bitch." … Isabel muttered after a while: "I never thought of it that way."

Isabel calmed down and Mary went to get her a cup of coffee, added some honey and cream to it, and handed it to her. Isabel took a few sips and then a few more and said: "Good coffee. Then she handed the cup back to Mary, had tears in her eyes and threw herself on the pillow saying: "He promised me love and a future. Now he is back with Ruth. When you see him tell him not to come back here.'

Mary held her hand and for the first time she felt close to her. After a while she said: "I have to go now, but I promise that I will be back every other day."

Isabel whispered: "I appreciate that."

As Mary headed for the door she noticed two pictures of women on the dresser who looked like saints but spirit-like. Next to them stood a glass of water.

"What are these two?"

"Two what?"

"These two paintings."

"Orishas … goddesses. Those are saints in our Santería tradition. The one in the light blue and white floating dress is Yemayá. The other one is Ochun, the goddess of honey. You ought to have a statue of Ochun in the garden for protection of your beehives."

"You believe in that?"

"Of course I do. It's our Cuban tradition. It is called Santería. You have pictures of saints in your church. Don't you?"

"You stirred my curiosity. That one protects bees?"

"She sure does, but listen Mary, I am so tired right now. I'll tell you all about it the next time you come."

"How about this weekend, Isabel?"

"Swell, this weekend. … Bye, Mary." Isabel's voice sounded weak and tired.

★★★

The Walshes were boiling and canning a mixture of apples and plums, enriched by a smidgeon of honey.

"Debbie, this small jar is for Isabel. I went to see her yesterday."

"Really, Mom?" Deborah almost dropped the ladle. "How did that go?"

"We made peace."

"That must have taken some will power."

"No, not really. That woman is lonely. She feels that Travis has deserted her after promising her paradise. I don't want to repeat what she called him after she heard that he had moved back in with Ruth."

"I can imagine."

"Debbie, she does not say so, but I can feel that she senses that she has very little time left on this planet. You should also pay her a visit. But tell me something. You may have come across it in Religious Studies. Ever heard of Santería?"

"Is she into that?"

"She says so, but what is it?"

"I am surprised that she of all people with her negative attitude towards blacks would hold on to Santería, but then I have heard it said that if you scratch the skin of a Cuban deep enough, a Santería believer will come out. She grew up in Cuba."

"Debbie, you are talking in riddles. What is it?"

"Okay, Mom. Santería is saint worship. Originally, it was practiced by African slaves in Cuba. They were from certain Nigerian tribes. The Spanish colonists would not allow their slaves to venerate their pagan saints. They had to accept the Catholic saints and were frequently forced into becoming Catholics. In order to uphold their native religious tradition, the Africans fooled the Spanish colonists by making it look like they had converted. They used pictures and statues of Catholic saints as fronts for their African saints. So, when the Spaniards saw them praying before a statue of Santa Barbara, the slaves may in reality have been praying to Obatalá. The Catholic statues also became fronts for their gods and goddesses, not only their saints, and the distinction between the two became very obscure. They called their deities and their saints 'Orishas.' Eventually, after slavery had been abolished, praying to Orishas spread to many white Cubans as well. That's it in a nutshell."

"Orishas. That is the term she used. Then she mentioned two other names, which sounded to me like something from a Voodoo religion. One was Ochún, the guardian of beehives."

"It may sound like that, but it isn't Voodoo. Nor is it devil worship, as some ignorant writers portray it. It is sincere faith in a set of gods and goddesses, saints and guardian angels. I don't know any more details but I could look it up."

"Don't bother. Just come with me when I bring her the preserves. She can then tell us all about the mermaid and the protector of beehives. I am very curious now."

"All right, I'll come along. My presence might spoil the visit for her."

"I don't think so. She wants to leave in peace. Let's go this Sunday afternoon."

Deborah let out a scream. "Holy Ochún, what is burning? The fruit stew is boiling over onto the rings. What a mess!"

Her mother grabbed two hot pads, pulled the large pot off the burner and shouted: "Ochún may be a good guardian of beehives, but she does a lousy job watching bubbling stew."

ALONE

"Nurse! … Nurse! …They cannot hear me. My voice is not strong anymore. I feel like screaming but I can't. … Nurse! … I cannot find the call button."

My throat is so dry. My chest hurts. I feel hot but I shiver. The green maple tree outside of my window is the only refreshing sight from this new room they gave me, and now I can hardly turn my head to see it. I love that tree. It must be a maple tree.

You must feel as lonely as I do. Are you afraid? I don't want to die. I am not even 40. Why does it have to be so early, God? They say that I smoked too much. The owner of the Starlight smokes more than I did, and he is 78. … Why me?

"Dear God, do you remember when I was speeding on the Lawrence Expressway during the rush hour and others were passing me up? Suddenly I saw flashing lights behind me. 'You have got to be kidding,' I told the cop when he handed me the ticket.

'Others are going faster. Why don't you go after them?' He told me that he clocked me at 65 miles in a 55- mile zone.

"Why me, Lord? There are many who smoked and drank more than I did. Why aren't you giving them cancer? I know. I know. I once heard a nun say: 'Don't blame God. You did it to yourself.' A rabbi who dropped in on me some time ago, -- he must have thought I was Jewish, -- said that I could turn my suffering into a great benefit for myself. "You can accept it as atonement for your sins," he said. "We accept pain from God and manage pain to obtain forgiveness." Easy for him to say that. He did not seem to have any pain. He was not facing death at 39.

Sins? ... I was mean to Deborah, I admit. I ruined her career. Every time I hear steps outside or a knock on the door, I dream that it might be Deborah, but it's only the nurse with more pain pills or a volunteer worker who coaches me into eating something. At the time I hurt Deborah I was driven by anger. Someone had told me that she was blaming me for the break-up between Travis and Ruth. I resented that. They called me a tramp and a slut, and she believed it. I ridiculed her after she talked to a tree. Here I am in this godforsaken room doing the same thing. That tree outside of my window is the only friend I have.

I am so sorry. I wish I could tell her. I wish she would knock on the door. I could make things right. What if she did? The thought frightens me. I would feel embarrassed. I always looked down on her and yet, she is so far above me. Apologizing? I have never been good at that. It's humiliating. Yemayá, please help me! Free me from this guilt-feeling which is following me into the next life! Deborah, where are you? I am so sorry. Her mother said that she would be back this weekend. Is it already the weekend? The last time Travis was here he no longer kissed me. Ruth despises me. Can you blame her? I am forgotten. Could Deborah forget me also? No, she couldn't, not after what I did to her. I am not forgotten. I am pushed aside. I am like a dead roach swept aside by a broom. Travis, you too must be guilt ridden, but you are too "macho" to admit it. Ruth? She probably says that I got what I deserve, that holier-than-thou woman. Unfortunately, she would not be entirely wrong.

Where are the priests, the ministers? Isn't it their job to pray with the dying and to console them? It is, ... but none of them knows me. How would they

know that I am here? I am not on anybody's list of friends. I am shoved aside.
I wish Deborah were here."

It is so hard to die alone. *"What are those shadows over there? Yemayá, is*
that you? I have always believed in you. Why don't you talk to me? Ochún,
why do you flit by like a shadow? A drop of honey, please! I am frightened. I
can't breathe. "God, can you forgive me if they don't? ... Can you? ... Please,
God! I feel so tired. I don't know how to pray, God. Nobody taught me. ...
God, please!" ... *I don't have the energy to pray. I am so tired ... so tired ...*
so weak ...

★★★

After the funeral Deborah remained for a while at Isabel's grave.

"Only five people came to see you off. We are all alone now and
we can talk. Travis came for just five or six minutes with a bouquet of
flowers, but he had nothing to say, no comments, no final expression of
friendship. That was the saddest part of it. Your brother Alfonso stayed
longer, but he had nothing to say either. A minister whom I had asked to
come spoke nicely and we all said the Lord's Prayer. '*Forgive us our trespasses*
as we forgive those who trespass against us.' Now everybody is gone and the
cemetery workers are waiting for me to leave so that they can lower your
casket, a plain wooden box made of clean pinewood. It looks and feels
warm. My mother paid for it. That is the kind of box I would like to have
after I am gone, none of those $2,000 to $5,000 metal shrines.

"Isabel, I hold no grudges. I was not fully aware of your condition.
I did not know that your cancer had progressed as far as it had. I would
have come to see you. I am certain you know that I am talking to you
now and that you understand me so much better now. I want to forget
the past. Forget? Well, that might be impossible. You remember how
people used to say: 'Deborah has an elephant's memory.' But I forgive,
and I promise you that I hold no grudges. I am not perfect either.
None of us is. One of my psychology professors used to say: 'When

people act against each other, in most cases their actions are a result of misinformation and misunderstandings.'

"You and I did not have a lot in common but we share one fate. People avoid me because of my looks. I am different. In the end they avoided you because of your condition and because you were different. They don't know what to say to a dying person. I was once at a party. I had actually gotten invited. Everybody was in a jovial mood when unexpectedly Louise showed up. Word had gotten around that doctors were giving her no more than two or three months. Suddenly there was silence. Two people broke the impasse by jumping up to offer her a chair as if she had not been able to pick a chair by herself. There were enough of them. Then there was silence again until one of my cousins asked her how her dad was doing. 'Oh, he is fine,' Louise answered. 'My mother is taking good care of him. I haven't seen him in a week. He often says that weeds don't die.' Then someone else said something like: 'This is the end of October and it's getting dark earlier. I hate to drive in the dark.' Someone else added: 'Me, too,' and both left acknowledging that they had really enjoyed the party. People don't know what to say to a dying person and they don't realize that someone like Louise would like to be treated like any other friend, not with artificial talk. That's why I would have liked to visit you and converse with you, but you slipped away. Isabel, let's become friends, you up there, I down here, and let's converse more often."

The sun was already setting. The cemetery workers came to finish their job and were obviously waiting for that strange woman to leave. As Deborah left she noticed a sea gull piercing the rose colored evening sky.

On the way home she crossed paths with three high school students smoking cigarettes on their way home from a ballgame. She walked up to them and said: "Girls, we just buried someone who died of lung cancer." The three gave her a puzzled look and after they had turned the corner and were out of sight, Deborah heard them laughing out loud.

MÉLISSA

I treasure the hours of my life I spent in observing and reflecting. Once I was sitting in a crabapple tree next to a playground. The blossoms radiated in the April sunshine. I was very tired and had to rest. A sister bee flew by hissing at me as if to say: "Get to work!" I hissed back: "Why do you sound so militant?" but she was already gone. I forgave her because she had acted in ignorance. She could not have known how tired I was. Ignorance is always at the bottom of hatred. Looking back, I can only say that all of us in the bee family should take out more time to reflect and meditate. Meditation is time well spent because our minds need it.

I must have stayed in that crabapple tree for a long time. Children came to play, six or seven year old angels. Two boys and one girl were white, two girls were Afro-American, and one boy was Asian. They played like sextuplets, completely oblivious to the color of their skin. Bees like to fly, kids like to run. One of the Afro-American girls stumbled and bruised her knee. Immediately, one of the two boys pulled out his hanky and wound it like a bandage around her knee and they all went on playing happily until one of the mothers announced that it was supper time. They did not like to, but they obeyed and each one ran home.

Why don't we play in our beehives or outside when we are just a few days old? Little dogs play, little cats play, but we never do. We derive pleasure from doing our chores: Feeding the larvae, feeding our brothers, feeding the queen, cleaning house, building combs, carrying out the dead, fanning to make the air circulate, and patrolling the entrance. All that and no play before the long awaited day comes for us to fly out into the orchards. We are happy doing our chores. It fulfills an inner craving, but after watching those children, I wish that we could be more like humans.

And yet, what is to become of those children when they reach their high school years and adulthood? Will they still get along? Will they perceive their daily tasks as burden and hardship? Will they still obey their parents? Will they respect the advice of the more experienced or laugh about it behind their backs?

Part III

"A nice porch you have here, Debbie," commented Edith who had unexpectedly dropped in for a visit. "Where are your parents?"

"My mom is taking a nap and my dad is socializing with his bees. He should not be doing this on a hot and muggy afternoon like this one. I told him so but he is a stubborn man, kind but stubborn, and a few beestings never seem to bother him. He does not even wear protective gear on a day like this."

"He then is somewhat like my dad, likewise kind and stubborn. He does volunteer work mowing the lawn at a kindergarten and at an orphanage where most kids aren't orphans but have been neglected. We told him not to do it this week because he twisted his back lifting the lawnmower in and out of his pickup-truck, but you might as well talk to a mule."

"What a coincidence that you would mention an orphanage. I visited Mercy Home yesterday to apply for a job. I would like to work with children. I told you why my plans for the diaconate have been shattered."

"You are a stubborn mule like our dads. I told you to switch to our church."

"Stubbornness in this case was good. The temptation was there, but if my appearance is not suited to face a congregation in the Episcopal

Church, why should it be any different in yours? I remember when our church got a new assistant pastor. For weeks parishioners commented on how handsome he looked. He was young and fresh out of the seminary and I overheard one young woman say: 'What a shame that I cannot date him!' What kind of comments would be whispered behind my back?"

"You know that you don't actually have to be ordained to function like a deacon or a minister."

"Did you read my thoughts or did I read yours? I had the same thoughts yesterday at the youth shelter. Those kids need guidance. They need theology talk on a child's or teenager's level. They have them there until they are 18. Some of them are rude and rough, I tell you. As a child, had I used their language talking to my parents, my ears would have been stretched until they resembled rabbit ears. I had been sure that I could do a lot of good at that home and have a job with benefits, but unlike the people at the Episcopal parsonage, who lightly and politely, but directly hinted at my problem, the director and the assistant at the youth shelter let me find out by myself.

'Just hang around for a few hours and supervise them while they are supposed to do their homework,' the director said to me. When I heard some of those 10 to 15 year old brats talk back at me, I could hear their drunken and dope-consuming parents talk, but that did not bother me much until I heard one of the high school age kids refer to me as that new witch with the funny chin, and another one burst out laughing. That's when I decided not to apply. In retrospect I think that I am a coward. The question is: Could I be a youth minister to them? The director seemed to have his doubts. Kids are open and can be cruel. And yet, when I see children being noisy and running around when they are supposed to be quiet, I am reminded of the gospel passage in which Jesus reprimanded his disciples after they had scolded the parents for bringing the children to be touched by Jesus:

'Let the children come to me and do not hinder them. It is to just like these that the kingdom of God belongs.'

"Yeah, but those were little kids not ridiculing Jesus' face," interrupted Edith. "What now?"

"I have decided to try one of the larger nursing homes, St. Francis, which has an ad in the church paper for a spiritual advisor. I am going there tomorrow."

"Good luck! I mean it. There won't be any giggling behind your back."

"Do you know that some of them hardly ever see their children? Maybe on their birthdays or at Christmas time. All the relatives will, however, be at their funerals."

"If they hire you, I'll treat you to a dinner at a cozy restaurant which I discovered. By the way, about my wedding …"

"There comes dad," Deborah interrupted.

"Good afternoon, girls. I did not know we had company."

"Dad, this is my friend Edith I told you about. What is the matter? You look nervous. Is something wrong?"

"There certainly is. We seem to have a major problem. I have never seen that many dead bees on the ground and live ones crawling like snails."

"Did you open a box to see what's what inside? Could it be the mites?"

"I opened two of them, lifted out several frames, and found absolutely nothing wrong inside. I have not yet looked into the brood chambers. Come and see for yourself."

Deborah and Edith were speechless when they saw the ground covered with a slow moving brown carpet. "You need to call the inspector, Dad."

"I'll do that. In the meantime, why don't you make us a pot of coffee?"

"Good idea. What is that pie tin doing under the apple tree?" asked Deborah.

"It probably got left there yesterday when Eric and one of his friends played here." Fred picked it up. "It's sticky and smells of honey," he said and threw the pie tin into the bee shed.

Mary was already in the kitchen, her eyes still a little sleepy, and when they told her about the bees, she was just as puzzled as Fred. As they were drinking coffee, Edith announced that she had actually come to tell them the date of her wedding and that they would receive an invitation in the mail.

"Who is the lucky fellow?" Mary asked.

"Elvis Shaker, he is a student at San Jose State majoring in Civil Engineering."

"Not a bad choice," said Fred.

"It is very considerate of you to want to invite us," remarked Mary.

"Well, you see, Mrs. Walsh, Debbie and I have been friends for two years now, ever since we ran into each other on the day of registration. Elvis and I have agreed on a simple wedding. Therefore we are inviting only relatives and close friends."

"We feel honored," answered Fred. "Thanks for including us."

Ruth was at home with Eric.

"Eric, what are my pie tins doing under your bed?"

"Me and David need them to collect rocks."

"David and I, Eric, not me and David. I did not know that you were now into rock collecting."

"In science class we learned all about rocks and the teacher asked us to look for small and unusual rocks and bring them to science class."

"I wanted to bake strawberry pies this morning and all of my pie tins were gone. I see you have only two here. Where are the others?"

"I don't know. I only took these two. Sorry, Mom."

"Next time, would you please ask?"

"Yes, Mom. You can have these back. Me and David can use lunch bags for our rocks."

"David and I, not me and David. I see that they are still clean. We will have two strawberry pies. Where are the other three?"

"I don't know, Mom."

The following afternoon the bee inspector came and spent two hours examining the beehives.

"Fred, what did the inspector have to say?" Mary asked that evening.

"We examined all six hives and lifted out the frames. He could not find anything wrong except for a lot of dead bees. He took a few pieces of comb from each box to the lab for analysis. We did notice some sweet smelling sticky substance on each landing platform. Bees don't do that. They are sticklers for cleanliness."

"How did it get there and what was it?"

"No clue. I remember that yesterday Debbie spotted a pie tin tossed under the apple tree. It had the same sticky substance on it. I took it out of the shed where I had thrown it and gave it to the inspector. So, when he calls, you know what he is referring to."

"Sure hope he comes up with an answer. If it is some new disease it could eliminate all honey production."

As Fred was about to get up, Mary said: "By the way, Fred, Debbie came up with one cuckoo idea. She is always concocting something. There is that nun in Calcutta by the name of Teresa. She is originally from Albania or one of those countries. She is creating a new order called 'The Missionaries of Charity.' They work with the poorest in the streets of Calcutta. Man, Debbie is considering joining them. Can you imagine her in those filthy streets being handicapped herself? I put it on thick and, hopefully, scared her out of it."

"Mary, she is not as handicapped as you make her out to be, but nevertheless, I would hate to have her that far away from us."

"She also mentioned St. Francis, the nursing home, but she pronounced the name Teresa of Calcutta as if it were something from the adventures of Huckleberry Finn."

"Well, you are the one who insisted on giving her the middle name Teresa. It is probably just one of those wild urges she often gets."

★★★

The following day the phone rang while Deborah was just about to leave the house to give a reading lesson to her very first student, Alma, who was still confined to the wheel chair. She could not and would not abandon her former ABC students. It was the inspector who called.

"This is Inspector Haberdink. May I talk to Mr. Fred Walsh please?

"Sorry, Mr. Walsh is not in right now. Can I give him a message? I am his daughter."

"Yes, would you please. Tell him that the lab tests show remnants of honey sprayed with DDT on both the pie tin and around the entrances of each beehive."

"Excuse my ignorance, Sir. I remember the acronym DDT from one of my chemistry classes, but I could never remember that tapeworm of a word for DDT.

"DDT is an illegal insecticide. It stands for dichlorodiphenyltrichloroethane. It was declared illegal two years ago."

"I'll stick to the acronym."

"Don't feel bad about it. I haven't met many chemists who know how to say it, let alone spell it. That stuff will kill any insect which inhales or ingests it, and to make things worse, we found traces of it in the honey combs making the honey unfit for human consumption."

"Thank God, we processed honey several weeks before this happened."

"All the frames must be removed from the boxes and must be disinfected before reinserting them. I would actually buy new frames and start from scratch. You can buy frames with the foundation already built in and save the new bees time and effort. It is not too late in the season, and your dad knows that the bees need plenty of sugar water for the first two or three weeks."

"What about the bees which are still alive?"

"They are not going to last long. Consider them a total loss."

"New frames with foundation, new colonies. There goes the money from selling our honey."

"There are worse things in life, young lady."

"What makes you think that my dad wants to start all over?"

"Young lady, once the bees have gotten under your skin and into your blood, you will always be a beekeeper. Tell your dad to call me at any time."

"Sure will, and thank you, Mr. Haberdink, for getting to the bottom of this."

"We haven't reached the bottom yet. Question is: Who did it?" For that reason I am keeping the pie tin to have the lab examine it for fingerprints. We might never find the person. Did you ever find the person who some time ago stole your mother's jewelry?"

"No, no trace of him. We think that it might have been a teenager, but we have no suspect."

"You see, we might never get to the bottom of this one either. I have to hang up now, Miss Walsh. Bye."

Who would do a thing like that? "There are worse things in life, young lady," Mr. Haberdink had said. Don't I know it! I have to call Alma and cancel the session. I need to find Dad because time is now of the essence if he wants to start new hives. I know that the bees have gotten under his skin and into his blood.

MÉLISSA

Let me reminisce on just one more event in our family, in the good old days before I was born, days that weren't always so good. Our aunts told us about this rather greedy beekeeper who thought that, just because he owned my ancestors, he also had the right to starve them to death. At that time they were located near the High Sierras where snow and ice rule in January. Later the beekeeper shipped them to our present location between orange groves.

In September, so they reported, the beekeeper removed all of their honey-filled frames, even some from the brood chamber where we still had babies developing, all out of greed to sell more honey. He did not care if our ancestors made it through the winter. He replaced the frames with empty wafers. He gave us one dish of sugar water, then he forgot about us. As tempting as it was to get away from the s.o.b., there was no sense in moving out that late in the season in search for a hollow tree or a hollow wall in some house because they would have had to build all new combs from the beginning. Well, they worked overtime, both young and old, to bring home the little nectar and pollen that could still be found. Their motto was: Never give up!

That is what our ancestors bequeathed to us, never to give up. Many of them were not so lucky. Their souls were carried away before the sweet aroma of spring could come to their rescue. By March, their population had dwindled down from, maybe, 30,000 to 2,000, but our ancestor family survived. Bees embedded in amber found by entomologists in China suggest that we have been around for 50,000,000 years. I remember one of our aunts say: "No matter what humans do to us, we will be here for eons to come. We were, of course, lucky in that we had a very healthy queen who in the spring was able to lay eggs as fast as we could build pockets. Even after our souls move into the sunset, we will always remain in your memory and you will always remain in your children's memory."

Thus ended their story and I can still hear their whisperings today. In my mind I will always be with our offspring, with the strong and healthy ones as well as the ones who become victims of frosts, fires, or human greed.

HOPE REBORN

It was Friday, evening again, one of those quiet times which the Walsh family cherished when watching the sunset. Deborah was sitting by herself this time with her eyes fixed on the oak-tree that looked somewhat reddish in the parting evening sun. Her maternal grandfather had planted that tree when he was still young as part of a one-acre plot of oak trees long before the house was built on it. He had thought of a small oak tree forest as an investment for his grandchildren because in those days oak was very much in demand by manufacturers of furniture. Most of the trees, however, were felled much too soon. The trunk of the one on the front lawn, however, was like a pillar in a Gothic church. It had weathered many storms and a bunch of sparrows zigzagged noisily from branch to branch.

From where Deborah was sitting she could also see the beehives. *Who would do a thing like that?* "But then, they are just bees," someone said to *me a few days ago. Are there not thousands of human beings who fare no better?*

Deborah had thought of joining the Peace Corps which President Kennedy had established in 1961 to help the poverty stricken and underdeveloped areas of the world. More than once had she been tempted to apply, not only to help but also for the excitement of adventures in Paraguay or Timbuktu. Bee colonies always find a way to survive, she thought. Sparrows survive even on platforms of train stations, be it in Moscow or in Los Angeles, but humans in underdeveloped areas need our help. She envisioned herself in a bamboo hut at the Amazon teaching children reading and writing. But then, which Peace Core Office would even consider her when noticing her limp?

Debbie and Julie, those two sympathetic Mormon missionaries, who had returned several times, had suggested other avenues. It was obvious that they meant well, but it was also obvious that their goal was conversion.

I like them a lot, she thought. *They are genuinely friendly, intelligent and convincing at times because of their deep faith. I am kind of a coward. Or is it politeness? I have only lightly hinted at the problem I have in leaving my church. I cannot believe that the Book of Mormon, published in 1830, inspirational as it is, should be considered the "Word of God" on equal footing with the Bible. I also believe in apostolic succession in the Catholic and Orthodox Churches and in the validity of the Eucharist. And last but not least, the Mormon Church like ours, will not let women enter the circle of the clergy. Men make all the decisions. What would I gain by switching? I must work up the courage and tell them next time they come. I do not want them to waste their precious time on a mule like me.*

And yet, they have given me much courage and inspiration. I would never have heard about the two Deborahs in the Old Testament. They, too, were handicapped. In those days women were confined to family, home and kitchen, but they found important roles to fulfill in society. Could I be a nurse like the Deborah who now rests under the Oak of Crying? No school for nurses would consider me. Could I become a judge like the Deborah in the Book of Judges? My face would scare the guilty one, -- which would not be altogether bad, -- but nobody would elect me to that post. How did those women get to their positions?

When I called Fr. X. a few days ago, he mentioned an opening for a counselor at the Villa St. Francis that I had heard about. He thought that fitted in with my education. Fat chance, but I'll give it a try. Never give up! I bet that those two Deborahs had that as their motto. Bees never give up. Those sparrows out there never give up. Why should I?

★★★

Saturday morning Deborah went to the Villa St. Francis, a nursing home with 220 beds, which was operated by Franciscan sisters. In its earlier days, when it was smaller, half of the personnel were sisters, but now only seven were left, two of them over 70, trying hard to keep the Franciscan spirit alive. The full time position, which they had advertised, was for a "Spiritual and Bereavement Counselor and Coordinator of Cultural Programs." Quite a handful of scary assignments, Deborah thought. Nevertheless, she actually got excited about it, applied, was interviewed, and was offered the position. She first could not believe it and had to read the letter three times to be sure. "Edith, you owe me a dinner at that restaurant," she said out loud.

On her first morning, the director of the nursing home, Sister Mary Louise, showed her the facility and introduced her to every station. Since Deborah limped and walked with a cane, many of the patients and one of the nurses thought that she was being admitted. Before lunch Sister Mary Louise said to her: "Today you may either have lunch with the office staff or you may join a party in the courtyard. They are going to celebrate the 100th birthday of Mrs. LeDoux, one of our patients. She is quite alert for her age, and she has invited her entire Afro-American family, about 20 of them."

"I think, I'll join the party in the courtyard," Deborah answered to Sister Mary Louise's surprise. Afterwards, Sister said to the secretary who had accompanied them: "That is a courageous woman."

Little by little the relatives came dribbling in and gathered around Granny, as they called her, hugging, kissing, and wishing her well. She was a first class patient with a private room and the house was providing the beverages, hamburgers, hotdogs and a salad, a rare benefit for special visitors at nursing homes. The relatives brought the dessert items, all of which were granny's favorites. Deborah, after introducing herself to the grandmother as the new spiritual director, chose to sit at a table with five teenagers who soon began to pull out their cigarettes.

"Do you mind?" asked one of the boys.

"I cannot forbid you to smoke," answered Deborah. "All I can tell you is that not too long ago we buried a woman who at the age of 40 was diagnosed with lung cancer. She had started to smoke at 16 and had become a heavy smoker. If that does not frighten you, go right ahead."

"One won't kill us," said one of the girls, and two of the five lit up. The others seemed to be too embarrassed in the presence of Miss Walsh and resisted the temptation.

"Are you a nun?" asked one of the boys.

"No, I am not, but the idea is tempting. I am new here, and my job is to help any patient who is down in the dumps."

"Will you get paid for that?" asked one of the girls who had lit up first.

"How much?" asked another.

"I am not really doing it for the money. Of course, I'll get paid like anyone else who works here, whatever nursing homes pay, but the real satisfaction comes from having made the day of a patient a little more cheerful. You would be surprised to see how many of these old people are not as lucky as your grandmother. They never receive any visitors. They are lucky if someone sends them a birthday card or Christmas greeting. They are the ones who need to know that somebody cares." *Now I am talking as if I had been working here for years*, Deborah thought.

"You mean they don't have any relatives or is it that their relatives don't give a damn?"

"Both," answered Deborah as more guests arrived.

There were not enough chairs and Deborah offered hers to one of the new arrivals. He happened to be an uncle of some of the teenagers and he only accepted after she insisted. She began to walk around from group to group, conversing and leaning on her cane. The uncle said to the smokers: "That funny looking woman walks with a cane and she offered me her seat." He waved at her and offered her back the seat but she answered: "Don't worry about me, sir, I need the exercise.

My condition worsens if I sit too much. You just stay here and enjoy the day."

"Quite a woman," he remarked after she left. "Quite a lady," he corrected himself.

During lunch, after saying good-bye to the uncle and the teenagers, Deborah talked to Mrs. LeDoux once more and left because she would have felt awkward eating while standing up. She had a drink from the cold-water fountain and headed for the office of Sr. Mary Louise.

"How were the hamburgers?" sister asked. She always prided herself on the high quality food her institution served.

"They were fine. I had nice conversations with the guests."

"If you want to get your feet wet, go and see Mrs. Wilber in room 205," sister suggested. "She has been crying a lot lately and we have not been able to figure out why, except that she has suffered a mild stroke and that she has terminal cancer. Doctors give her a few years. She is only 58. Later we have to sit down with our activities director and plan the weekend."

"Sister, you must have had several or, maybe, many applicants for this position. Why did you hire me?"

Sister Mary Louise thought for a moment and, looking at a pile of manila folders, which looked like job applications, she said: "There are a lot of patients here who need someone like you. They need your experience with pain."

Deborah thought of what Deborah the Mormon missionary had said and went to room 205.

★★★

Fred, Angie, and Eric wore their beekeeping outfits on this Saturday because they had to transfer the bees to new boxes and Fred had said that the bees would not take too kindly to that. Fred had bought six new boxes with new frames with foundation, some containing honey as a bait. He had placed the new boxes in front of the old hives, opening to opening.

"We have to transfer the queens into the new boxes and all other bees will eventually follow. They got busy with the first one and lifted out some of the old frames in the upper boxes and set them in front of the new box. They were not covered with bees that looked like a brown moving carpet. There may have been 20 or 30 on each frame. Apparently, most of the remaining bees had abandoned the upper boxes and congregated in the brood chamber. Grandpa carefully lifted the grid that separates the brood chamber. There they were, on top of each other. Since no honey had ever been extracted from the brood chamber, those frames were heavy.

"Do we have to throw away all of this honey?" asked Eric.

"I am afraid so. Small traces of DDT may have gotten into the combs from around the entrances and the pie tin, but it is not very likely because these bees did not get in touch with the DDT, otherwise they would be dead by now. These are the younger bees who have never been outside of the hives, not even on the platform. We have to play it safe, though. Mr. Haberdink thought that they would all be dead by now.

"Who would do that to bees?" asked Angie.

"I don't have a clue," answered Fred. They found the queen. Grandpa carefully grabbed her from behind and placed her onto a new frame with honey in the new brood chamber. He added another honey-filled frame next to it. All the other new frames were already in the box. He put a new screen on top of the brood chamber and one upper box on top.

"Now we wait and see," he said. "The bees will start moving soon because they want to be with their queen. The number of bees has shrunk to a dangerously low level. We have five boxes to go."

Angie noticed a smile with a smirk on Eric's face. "It is not a laughing matter," she said in a very serious tone of voice.

"I was not laughing about losing the bees," he whispered to Angie. "Grandpa's fly is open and I saw a bee crawl in."

"Eric!" shouted Angie.

"Come on you two. Let's get this done," said Fred and went to the next beehive. "We are lucky that a nice beekeeper friend gave us a dozen honey-filled combs. Angie, go into the house to see if grandma has the sugar water ready."

Mary and Angie came back with a pitcher of sugar water, enough for six colonies. Suddenly Fred jumped, let out a scream and ran into the bee house. Mary followed him and the children heard her yell: "Fred, what are you doing there. Do you have to go so badly? Is it your prostate again? – She came out after a while and said: "He got stung in a sensitive spot." Now even Angie could not hide a grin on her face.

To do the remaining boxes took until evening. At the supper table Fred said: "Aren't we lucky that all six queens are alive? It is too late in the year to have the bees get used to new ones." Then he opened the table drawer and took out two small white cardboard boxes with transparent covers. "Angie and Eric, I made these for you. You can show them to your science teacher." Inside each little box, pinned down with bobby pins, were a dead queen, a few worker bees, and one drone. Fred had saved the dead queens from a year ago, when he had to re-queen several hives. "You can explain to your class the function of these bees. Right, Eric? Now you have a good foundation.

A good foundation. He sounds just like mom. He had to use that awful word, but I might get an "A", Eric thought.

A car door slammed on the driveway. "Must be Debbie," said Mary. "Someone must have given her a ride."

After a while Deborah came waltzing in swinging her cane around. "I like my new job. This was a perfect day." She yelled it and Mary said:

"Debbie, we are not hearing impaired like some of your new friends who refuse to wear hearing aids."

"Anything left for me to eat? Haven't had anything since breakfast except for a cup of coffee and some cookies at the planning session."

"No lunch?" asked Eric.

"No Eric, no recess, no lunch."

"And I thought that my school was bad. We have recess and lunch."

"Eric, I envy you, but it was a perfect day nonetheless. What have you all been up to?"

Fred, looking tired, leaned back in his chair and answered: "We set up the new boxes and transferred the queens. Hopefully, the bees will follow. The population is down to a critical level. Kids, once the bees have relocated themselves, we must not forget to move the old boxes out of sight. We don't want the bees to move back into the old ones."

"Dad, Mr. Haberdink said that the old colonies had to die out or be destroyed." Deborah sounded concerned.

"I don't believe that," commented Fred. "If the remaining bees had ingested DDT, they would all be dead or dying by now."

"I hope you are right, Dad."

"Trust me, Queen."

Fred had some wine left in his glass. Deborah lifted it and said: "Long live the bees. Long live the Queens!"

The phone rang. When Deborah ran to answer it, Mary said to Fred and the children: "I wonder what happened at St. Francis. She hasn't been this hyper in a long time."

════ MRS. WILBER AND OLD JIMMY ════

Deborah was well liked as a spiritual and bereavement counselor and the Franciscan sisters appreciated and respected her. Only visitors usually thought that she was one of the patients and children often stared at her. The staff had noticed her cheerful and uplifting way with patients who suffered from depression or simply from loneliness. The sisters had also noticed a deep spirituality in Deborah, coupled with some rather progressive views in theology. Amazingly, it was some of the older sisters who felt and thought along the same lines as Deborah did. They, too, felt that women had been relegated to serve a male hierarchy. Why could they not be deacons at least? Deborah was surprised and impressed.

At Sr. Mary Louise's request, Deborah had visited Mrs. Wilber in room 205 and that visit had been a new start for Mrs. Wilber. That lady had been crying on and off but the staff could not figure out why. She had a private room and her own TV-set. What else could a patient want?

"Good morning, Mrs. Wilber. I'm Deborah Walsh. Do you remember me from last week?"

"I sure do. What brings you back?"

While shaking Mrs. Wilber's hand Deborah said: "I enjoyed your company and our conversation last week so much that I wanted to start off today on a good note."

"Can I take that as a compliment?"

"You sure can."

"That's the first time since I came here that someone has paid me a compliment. They only ask: 'What's bugging you today?' They don't ask if I would like to talk. Often I have a hard time getting the right words out and they are all too busy to sit down and wait for that."

"Yes, Mrs. Wilber, they are very busy and often the home is understaffed, but I have enough time this morning. What if I made the two of us a cup of tea and we could enjoy each other's company and take our time talking?"

"I would like that very much."

After Deborah had left to prepare the tea, Mrs. Wilber had tears in her eyes, and if one of the staff had been listening at the door, she could have heard her say: "I can tell by looking at that young woman that she, too, must have had her trials."

Deborah came with raspberry tea on a tip from the station nurse.

"Miss Walsh, I see that we two have the same taste."

"I thought so all along," answered Deborah.

Mrs. Wilber took a few sips and said: "Hmm." This is going a lot better than I had expected, thought Deborah and said: "Mrs. Wilber, why don't you call me Debbie and I'll call you Annette. My family always calls me Debbie."

"Yes, let's do that."

"Annette, I bet that you have been through a lot in your life. No need to tell me everything, but what were some of the worst happenings in your life and what were some of the nicest?"

"I'll tell you mine if you tell me yours." Annette sounded curious.

"It's agreed." Deborah agreed with a feeling of trepidation because this could easily take up all morning. At 11:00 she had to see Jimmy in 210.

"I'll make it short," said Mrs. Wilmer as if she had sensed Deborah's problem. "I have a boy and a girl. The boy is 28 and the girl is 26. We belong to the Baptist Church. When the children were little, my husband was falsely accused of murder. He was framed. He also had a bad heart condition. When hope for parole was shattered, he suffered a major heart attack and died in the jail's infirmary. Three months later he was acquitted of all charges. The children were 10 and 12. I could only find minimum wage jobs for many years and many a night I cried myself to sleep because sometimes I did not know where the food for the next day would come from or how to pay for new shoes for the children. The Salvation Army was a godsend. They did so much for us.

By the time my son was a senior in high school, he became an I-know-it-all snob. He only accepted advice from his friends and no longer went to church because they had told him that church was for children and old women. To this day, even though he studies at a church affiliated university, he comes to church with me only occasionally, when it fits into his schedule. He claims that he has too much studying to do. But I know that he spends a lot of time socializing with his friends while telling me that he is at the library, by phone that is. Little time to visit me. That's my son Leicester. I still love him dearly, and that's why it hurts.

"Your son's name is Leicester?"

"That's him. The name Leicester has been in our family for generations way back in old England."

"It's a nice name."

"Can you take more?"

"Get it off your chest. That's what I am here for."

"After he stopped going to church the next blow came. My daughter Lynn. When she was about 17, I noticed that money was disappearing from my purse. She, too, stayed out many nights telling me that she was reviewing for tests with her friends. Little by little it became clear to me that she was taking drugs. She denied it for some time, even sounded hostile when I wanted to sit down with her to discuss it. That went on until the next disaster struck: She was pregnant. Being opposed to abortion, -- I am a Baptist, you know, -- I talked her out of that, and during her pregnancy her attitude toward me changed. She realized that she needed me. She then let me help her raise the child who is now a strong, lively, and at times mischievous boy. We named him Alex."

"Thank God for that! What about her drug problem?"

"Good things do happen. During pregnancy she consented to enter a drug rehabilitation program, and it seems that to this day she has stayed clean. She never finished high school, though. At 20 she married a nice watch repairman who has pushed her into studying for the high school equivalency exam. Since she has always been allergic to books, that might take a while, but she is not opposing it either.

"Is she getting child support from Alex's father?"

"Don't you wish! She does not even know for sure who the father is."

"Annette, I see what you have been going through. Thank God, you kept your head above water. You are a strong woman."

"When they are little, they kick us in the womb. When they get older they kick us in the heart." I once read that in a 19th century German novella called *Die Judenbuche (The Jewish Beech Tree)."*

"I did not know that you read German."

"I don't. It was a translation."

"Now everything seems fine again."

"On the surface, yes. Now and then they come to visit, … now and then, … and bring me flowers. Last time little Alex asked me to read him a story. For once I felt like a grandmother. Neither Leicester nor Lynn attends church. Why is God doing this to me? I prayed all my life and I tried to set a good example. I wonder if He hears me."

Deborah sat on the bed next to Mrs. Wilber and took her hand. "Annette, God's calendar is different from ours. He has a different timetable. Leicester and Lynn are still young. A lot can happen in the years to come. Your prayers are not in vain. Things will get better. Never give up because I know that God never gives up on any of us. He will never give up on Lynn and Leicester."

"But I won't see it. With my cancer I don't have forever."

"You will see it from above much better than you could ever see it now."

"You think so?"

"I do."

"Well, I forgot to mention that a couple of weeks ago Leicester came to see me and told me about a term paper he had written for art history about a sculpture of Mary, the mother of Jesus, about her facial expression, and the trauma watching her son maltreated and killed. He said that some other student had given him some good pointers for the paper. He also explained to me about communion and the consecrated bread and wine. So, maybe, you are right. Maybe, something is brewing in him."

"That, Annette, is the best news you have given me all morning. You see, God works in his own ways. Never give up! … Oh my, it's already 11:00 o'clock. I have to leave now but I'll be back for tea soon. I promise."

"You were going to tell me about *your* troubles. You promised. Remember?"

"I do remember and I'll fulfill that promise, even though my troubles are nothing compared to yours. I'll tell you next time I come. I promised someone else that I would visit him at 11:00."

"Got a boyfriend?"

"Sort of. Old Jimmy down the hall."

"Then run but come back."

"Promise."

Deborah left puzzled by her discovery. *How dumb of me that I never asked Leicester about his last name! He never mentioned his mother. What was he trying to hide? That she was disappointed in him? I wonder if he ever inquired about my last name. I need to have a talk with him about visiting his mother. It seems that what I told him in the area of theology actually stuck.* Running she whispered: "God chose me as his instrument."

★★★

Old Jimmy down the hall was not feeling well today and he was very slow in chewing and swallowing the bits of food that one of the aides was trying to shove into his mouth. She seemed to be in a hurry and displayed little patience. Deborah looked on for a minute and said to the aide: "I'm sure that you are very busy during lunch time. Why don't I feed him today?"

"Thanks, Miss. Walsh. I have to help two others with their lunch. I appreciate it."

Deborah gave Jimmy plenty of time to chew and to swallow. She did it with so much tenderness that during a friendly chat after lunch Jimmy asked her if she could come back the next day and feed him again. "This was the first meal I enjoyed in three days," he said. "No one around here has enough time for an old snail like me."

"I'll try to fit it in," said Deborah and fluffed up his pillow. "Would you like a piece of honey cake with your lunch tomorrow?"

"I love honey. I used to raise bees. I had 10 hives until a fire destroyed them."

"How did that happen?"

"The grass on the hill on which they were located was dry. It was the middle of July. The wooden shack in which the hives were housed was gone in no time. The fire department suspected lightning as the cause because shortly before one could hear thunder for half an hour. I felt devastated. The bees had been my psychiatrists."

"Were you able to get started again?"

"Yes, some nice Irish fellow, much younger than I, gave me two of his hives. I am not sure anymore, but I think his name was Fred. He did not have that many hives himself, but he refused to let me pay him. That's how I got started again."

Deborah could not believe her ears. Two incidences in one morning! After a friendly chat and a promise to bring him honey cake the next day, she stopped at the chapel and said: "God, you have shown me that you meant for me to be here. I accept the calling."

Late that night she asked her dad about what old Jimmy had told her and he confirmed the story. He explained: "I could not take any money from him. That man was poor, and I mean poor. He had no family and had battled a lot of health problems. Years later he suffered a stroke and the sisters took him into the nursing home even though his social security check pays only a portion of the cost."

The next day, when Deborah brought Jimmy a piece of honey cake, she and Jimmy became best friends. Annette had been right in her suspicion.

THE WEDDING

Edith and Elvis had decided on a simple wedding in their hometown of Morgan Hill, mainly to save Edith's parents money because they were making great financial sacrifices sending her to a private university. Furthermore, Elvis and his father had never been much for fancy formalities. The mere wearing of a tuxedo would have constituted a sacrifice. They were more of the rodeo types. In fact, Elvis had once told Edith in reference to something he had heard in an American Literature class at San Jose State University, that Ernest Hemingway impressed him because he did not travel to Oslo to receive his Nobel Prize. Elvis was convinced that it was because Hemingway would have had to wear a tuxedo. Hemingway's parents had been extremely Victorian and he had broken with tradition in several ways early on after returning from Italy in 1919, having been an ambulance driver for the Italian Red Cross in the service of the Italian army toward the end of WWI. Thereafter he would never have paraded around in a tuxedo. That made Elvis fall in love with Hemingway.

The altar of the Methodist church, however, was tastefully decorated with two rather expensive flower baskets, and on the altar teble there were two candles made of pure beeswax, a wedding present from Deborah. They were already lit and their sweet aroma permeated the small church.

Before the ceremony, Edith spotted Deborah with her parents and waved at them. In her bridal gown and behind the silky veil she resembled a Madonna in romantic paintings. Elvis, on the other hand, had his necktie on crooked, and with his scruffy beard and his long brownish hair blown by the wind, he would have been the most perfect choice to play Robinson Crusoe in a movie.

"I am afraid we may have more than 50 guests here," Deborah heard one of the servers in the community room say as they were preparing for the reception. "We need more paper plates and cups." Deborah asked if she could help, but they told her that they did not want to impose on a guest. In one corner of the community room Deborah noticed the table for the presents. She placed her envelope on that table which was already loaded with neatly wrapped boxes. Being short on cash, she had written a poem about two candles instead of buying a present. The two wax candles on the altar and the poem would, hopefully, mean more than another crock-pot or blender. Among the many boxes Deborah saw a little package from her parents and a letter from Angie.

That girl is still into letter writing. It does not matter to her who the people are to whom she writes, as long as she receives an answer from them. Having had to buy dozens of 8-cent postage stamps, her piggy bank sounded empty the last time I dropped a quarter into it. I love that girl!

On the way out of the community room, when Deborah was still in the doorway, she heard one of the women say to another: "How did she get in here? Good grief!" Deborah spontaneously turned around and her eyes remained fixed on the two volunteers. One of them mumbled something and disappeared into the kitchen where she stayed for a long time until Deborah turned and left. A wonderful feeling of revenge overcame Deborah.

Coming back from the community room she spotted Leicester standing in the hallway.

"Leicester, nice to see you here. I did not know Edith had invited you."

"She didn't, and I am not staying for the reception. I just had to see her once more, - in her wedding gown."

"Do I detect a romantic feeling for her?"

"Very much so. You never noticed that, nor did she, but ever since our first brief meeting in the cafeteria on the day of registration, I have not been able to get her out of my mind. Because I was married and noticing that she already had a relationship, I did not pursue it, I did not even show it."

"You were playing with fire, but you controlled it. I feel very honored that you share your most personal feelings with me. I don't know how wise it was for you to come here and see her when she looks as pretty as today. It will make things only harder for you."

"I guess so, but I had to."

"Listen, Leicester. Since we have 15 minutes before the ceremony starts, I can tell you something. It will take only a few minutes. A couple of days ago I finally found out your last name. It puzzles me that I never asked you in spite of our lengthy theological conversations."

"How did you find out?"

"I met a very charming lady at St. Francis. You jerk, you never told me that she was in a nursing home."

"I see that you are not just an expert in religion, you also are a master spy," he answered kind of jokingly.

"Leicester, this is serious. You need to visit your mother more frequently. She feels lonely. Nobody there has much time for her. You don't know what it is like to be cooped up between four walls for several years and no one to talk to."

"I was there three weeks ago and spent two hours with her. She refuses to eat in the dining room. That's why she is cooped up in her room."

"What about last week? What about yesterday? Both you and Lynn should each go at least once a week. It's not as if you lived far away and had no car. Three miles is nothing."

"Well, ... what can I say? I guess you are right. Every three weeks is not enough. How come the staff there does not converse with her? What are we paying for?"

"Man, you have no idea how busy they are, and most of all, there never is a substitute for conversing with your own children."

"What were you doing there?"

"I work at St. Francis. I just started there as someone who talks to lonely souls, or better, as someone who listens to them."

"Is that a full time job?"

"I started only a few days ago and already found out that it is a one and a half time job. I also plan activities for them."

"I could see her tomorrow."

"You deserve a hug for that. Give yourself enough time with her, but don't tell her that I talked to you. You came to see her because you wanted to see her. That will make her day. Afterwards look or ask for me. I can pretty much make my own hours because I put in a lot of overtime. They have a neat cafeteria. ... My, I think it's time to go in. The ceremony is about to start."

The two joined Deborah's parents in the chapel. Robinson Crusoe was already standing next to the minister. The organist, whom Leicester recognized as a former classmate and music major, started the wedding march. Edith's father, a tall and fine looking gentleman, escorted her up the center aisle. The ceremony was nicely done, but Deborah felt that the minister's memorized text consisted of the same stereotype and worn-out wording that one hears at 95% of all weddings.

I wonder when the churches and wedding chapels will ever come up with something innovative. If I were a deacon, priest or minister, -- wishful dreaming, -- I would for instance include a candle ceremony with three candles. One would represent Christ who stated of himself: "I am the light of the world. He who follows me will not walk in darkness." Then I would light a second candle from the flame of Christ's candle and give it to the bridegroom who would face the bride and say something like: "Edith, as this candle consumes itself giving light, let me do the same for you throughout our lives." A third candle would then be lit from the Christ candle and be given to the bride. She would face the groom and say something like: "Elvis, as the flame of my love is burning now, let it always shine for you throughout our lives." A reading would follow from Matthew 5,14 ff or a similar text.

Love is a mysterious thing. What is it that draws two to each other? Planets and entire galaxies are drawn to each other by gravity; but what is gravity really? Scientists can give us only partial explanations. That's how it is with love. How can one explain the nature of psychological gravity? Why does A feel drawn to X but B does not?

I could also think of a rose ceremony and still keep the original ring ceremony. Yes, the ring ceremony needs to be kept. A ring with no beginning and no end is too significant an allegory for never ending love to be dropped. All the clergy would have to do is to use a little imagination, but this ceremony went like a million others with phrases, which are repeated mechanically and too often without consequences.

After the ceremony Leicester said good-bye to Deborah and left. He seemed to be fighting tears. He sat in his car for five minutes looking at the entrance to the parish hall and Deborah was afraid he might come back, but then he took off.

At one point during the reception Edith took the microphone, asked Deborah to come up and introduced Deborah as her best friend from college. "Best friend?" a woman asked the lady next to her at the table. She almost dropped the piece of the wedding cake off her fork. "I think that she is one of those nutty patients at St. Francis," the woman answered. "I have seen her there limping through the hallways. From the way she looks you can tell that she lacks a few marbles." At that point Robinson Crusoe gave Deborah a hug and a kiss. "Can you believe that?" the other woman asked. "I am sure glad he ain't my son-in-law."

Toward the end of the reception the new couple performed what seemed to be a well-rehearsed dance while students from the university provided the music. Edith then asked her father for a dance while Elvis asked his mother. Edith and her father circled around on featherlike feet like professional ballroom dancers with elegance and symmetry. Meanwhile Elvis shook his mother back and forth like in a wagon train dance at the western frontier. She seemed to enjoy it but almost lost her balance on the way back to her table. Then followed the dances of Elvis with his mother-in-law and Edith with her father-in-law whereby the two ladies did not fare much better than Elvis' mother had. Deborah enjoyed watching the dances and was, of course, not asked for a dance herself, not even later on when the dance floor got crowded. A blessing in disguise, she thought, never really having learned to dance. At the same time she envied the others. Nature had deprived her of aspiring to achieve such athletic and artistic heights. She had been called to a different kind of perfection, and weighing the two against each other, her feeling of envy little by little subsided.

THE MYSTERY

Angie was very quiet at the supper table. She ate very little and Ruth could tell that something terrible was bothering her. After supper she joined Angie in her bedroom. Angie was lying on her bed face down. Ruth put her hand on her shoulders and said: "Angie, you know that whatever you choose to tell me will remain strictly between you and me if you want it to be that way."

Angie turned around and said: "I was in Eric's room today looking for my binoculars which he borrowed from me a long time ago. I thought that they might be in his toy trunk which he calls his treasure chest. There they were, but there is also something else in that chest, a spray can that says DDT on it."

Ruth almost went into shock. "That's all we need. God help us!"

"I cannot believe that it is something for his science class, but I did not want to bring it up at the dinner table."

"Science teachers would never put that stuff into a child's hands. Any science teacher knows that the use of DDT has been declared illegal."

Angie suggested: "Go to the treasure chest and see for yourself. That way he will not think that you got it from me. Could it be that he is still upset that we confiscated his slingshot and never returned it?"

"At this point there is no way of telling what motivated him to harm the bees, if he did it at all. It may just have been an innocent boyish prank. Let's not mention any of this to anyone until I have talked to Eric myself. First, I'll search his treasure chest while he is glued to the TV-set. In the meantime, pray for both Eric and me."

Ruth looked into Eric's treasure chest. For a moment she thought that the world went black before her eyes and she began to feel dizzy. But then she took a deep breath, pulled herself together to talk to Eric who was watching his favorite Disney program.

"Eric, I need to talk to you, upstairs in your room."

"Mom, I am in the midst of a movie."

"Eric, this cannot wait."

Eric followed his mother to his bedroom.

"Eric, do you remember when you took the pie tins?"

"Yes."

"How many did you take?"

"Two. I gave them back to you."

"Don't lie to me, Eric. Are you sure you did not take a third one?"

"I never took a third one."

"Yesterday you and Angie helped grandpa saving the bees. You know, therefore, why so many of them died."

"Grandpa said that someone poisoned them. Someone smeared honey on the landings and sprayed poison on them."

"Was the poison only on the landings?"

"I don't know."

"Did grandpa not mention something about a pie tin?"

"Yes, now I remember. He said that they found a pie tin under the apple tree."

"Do you know what the poison is called?"

"No, he didn't say.

"Maybe, this will refresh your memory." Ruth opened Eric's toy box and took out the spray can.

"Does this look familiar to you and do you know what this is?"

"I don't know what it is but I like the picture on it."

"Why do you like the picture?"

"This guy has strong arms and he is killing nasty insects."

"Do you think that bees are nasty insects?"

"Only when they sting you."

"This stuff is called DDT. See it here? Grandpa said that you and David had been playing in the yard behind the beehives the day before the bees began to die and that they found a pie tin with this kind of poison under the apple tree." At that Eric could only stutter as he answered. "Me and David did not do that."

"David and I."

"David and me … I … did not do it. I found this spray can under one of our rose bushes. I liked the picture on it. That's why I took it. It was empty. No spray came out when I pushed on the red button. I did not know that it was poison."

He started to cry and Ruth said: "I hope that you are telling me the truth." She took the spray can and went down to the kitchen. Someone had left the door to the food pantry open again. Before closing it, Ruth noticed that the honey jar, which had been started a week ago, was missing.

The next day Ruth talked to Travis about her suspicion: The pie tins, the missing honey jar, the DDT spray can in Eric's possession, and the fact that Eric and David had been playing behind the beehives the day before Fred discovered the disaster. "There is more than coincidence here," she said. "Did you say DDT?" Travis asked seemingly shaken up a little.

"Eric said that he found the can under a rose bush in front of our house."

"There is a simple explanation for that," explained Travis. "To get rid of those aphids, I sprayed the roses a week ago with DDT. DDT is the most effective insecticide. I may have forgotten to take the can back to the garage and left it under the roses."

"Was it empty?"

"There may have been a few drops left in it. I am not sure."

"Don't you know that the use of DDT is no longer permitted?"

"I know, but the hardware stores are still selling off leftover stock. What harm is there in using it up as long as you don't use it on fruit-producing plants or in vegetable gardens. Nobody eats roses, for heaven's sake."

"That is not entirely true. I used to make rosebud tea from our own roses."

"But you no longer do."

"There may have been enough left in the can to try it out on bees," Ruth continued after a while.

By now Travis was getting agitated and actually began to shout: "The whole thing is ridiculous. Why would Eric want to kill his grandpa's bees? Ludicrous idea. He probably does not even know what DDT is."

"Travis, as much as it hurts a mother, the evidence speaks for itself."

"Nonsense! It is ludicrous to suspect Eric. Your dad is very frank and outspoken. With his big mouth he has made himself enemies on several occasions. There may be guys out there who wanted to get back at him. Your old man has to learn to keep his trap shut."

While Travis sounded agitated Ruth remained calm and said: "Yes, my dad has always been straightforward, but he does not have a big mouth. There is simply no truth in that, and I don't believe that he has ever made enemies that way. You seem to know more than I do." At that Ruth turned around and went back into the house. Travis had turned toward his car and Ruth heard him say: "Damn!"

That evening Ruth could not sleep. She had reached a Y in the road and did not know which direction to choose. *Travis may have a point. Why would Eric do something like that? What kind of a mother am I to suspect my own child? Why did Travis get so agitated to the point of shouting at me? What is it that makes me suspect him all of a sudden? He has had a few rather sharp disagreements with my dad, and he will always resent the straightforward man-to-man talk like the one dad had with him after Travis and Isabel came back from Las Vegas.*

I need clarification; otherwise I might have a nervous breakdown. Tonight after supper I am going to wrap up the water glasses of both Eric and Travis. I am going to ask Mr. Haberdink to have both glasses tested for fingerprints and compare them with what might be on the pie tin that is still in the lab. I hope they can do that; if not, then at the police station. If the fingerprints don't match, no one will ever know that I did this, and I will remove the last doubts in my mind about Eric and Travis.

★★★

Eric and Travis were washing the old Pontiac when Eric asked: "Dad, why does everybody think that I did it?"

"Did what?"

"They think that David and I killed the bees."

"Nonsense, boy. Not everybody thinks that. I know that you didn't do it. I know that for a fact."

"But they think that I did it."

"Let them think what they want. You and I know that you would never do anything like that. They have no proof."

"They still have my sling shot."

"Why is that?"

"A long time ago Mom saw me aim at birds. Then Angie saw me aiming at a bee. She pulled the slingshot out of my hands and hid it. That's the last I saw of it."

Travis laughed out loud. Then he said to Eric: "Tell you what. Let them keep it. I'll make you a new one, much better than the one you had."

They were about finished washing the car when Travis asked: "Why do they think that you did it?"

"I took two of mom's pie tins for my rock collection for science class. She found them in my room. She said that more than two pie tins were missing. She also said that near the beehive, under the crabapple tree, grandpa found a pie tin that had honey and poison on it. They also found an empty spray can for DDT in my room. I had only picked it up in front of the house because I liked the picture on it. Me and David were playing behind the beehives the day before the bees began to die."

"So that's what it is," whispered Travis to himself. Then he put his arm around Eric and said once more: "Eric, you did not do it."

SELF-BETRAYAL

It was Labor Day and the Walshes had invited the Rileys and the neighbor with his wife and another beekeeper to a barbecue. Fred was at the grill. Mary was fixing the garden salad and Deborah was about done with the potato salad and the dessert. Travis and Ruth were supposed to bring the wine because Travis, employed at the Starlight, was supposed to be the wine connoisseur although at that place wine was seldom asked for. They made their money on whiskey, beer, and cheap cocktails. Everybody arrived except Travis. Ruth explained that he had refused to come along mumbling something to the effect that Fred and Mary did not like him. He did not want to spoil the party for the sake of the children. Travis' absence and his reasoning put a damper on the festive spirit, which had developed because the six bee colonies had been saved. The beekeeper had brought with him a few more frames with pollen and honey. After they had been inserted with Angie's and Eric's help, the drumsticks and the hamburgers were ready. Fred had also brought a bottle of Merlot from the cellar and Deborah had brought out the tape recorder for background music.

Unexpectedly, a cold west-wind drove a dark cloud over the area and the party had to be moved to the covered porch. Later that evening, after everybody had left and the table had been cleared, Fred asked Mary and Deborah to join him for a little longer on the porch. While stuffing his pipe with his favorite brand of tobacco, he said to Mary and Deborah: "I think I know why Travis did not want to show his face here. Two weeks ago he and I had a confrontation. I kept it to myself because I did not want Ruth to know. Chip Crome, Ernie's former partner, had told me that Travis was flirting and kissing again, this time with a brunette who hangs around the Starlight. I asked Chip whether he was absolutely sure that it wasn't just some foolish and harmless flirting. No, he said that it was fondling and deep kissing. I decided not to mention it to Ruth because I did not want to destroy their patched-up relationship, but I felt that it was my obligation to have a serious talk with Travis. I thought that if after talking to him he would stop the flirtations, it would be better if Ruth never found out. I also asked Chip not to say anything to anyone, at least not for now. Chip insisted that he had seen the smooching on two different evenings.

"So, I went to Ruth's house while the children were in school and she was at the diner. I talked to him in a nice and fatherly way about the rumors, which were beginning to spread about him and the brunette.

I said to him: 'Travis, I don't know the facts, and this might all be false rumors, but I wanted you to be aware of what people are whispering behind your back. If there is some truth to it, please be more careful for the sake of your marriage and the children whom you love. I have not mentioned it to anyone and it might all be false rumors, but if Ruth should mention it some day, be assured that she did not get it from me.'

"I wanted to say more but at that point he became agitated and with a belligerent look on his face he told me in no uncertain terms that the rumor was a lie and that his private life and matters of his family were none of my damn business. He said that he was tired of always being compared to me. 'You have always been the perfect one who landed good jobs and earned decent money,' he said. 'I am the failure who cannot provide. I am sick and tired of hearing it!'

He also said that now he had a good relationship with Ruth and the children and that he would not allow his in-laws to destroy it. 'But Travis,' I said, 'I have never compared you to me, and this conversation is strictly between you and me. I am not the one who is spreading the rumor. All I want is to save your marriage. You can trust me.' But he told me to stop worrying about him and his family and to keep my nose out his business.

'Okay,' I said. 'I'll keep my nose out of your business. If Ruth mentions it some day, she did not hear it from me. You can trust me on that. I just wanted to help. Some day, when Angie is married, you will, I hope, be just as concerned about her as I am about Ruth and the children.'

"I tried to shake hands with him but he refused and said: 'You take care of your bees and let me take care of my family.' At that he got into his truck and took off with tires screeching."

There was dead silence until Deborah broke the impasse by saying: "I always felt that there still was common sense and a nice streak in him, but his reaction might indicate that there is something between the brunette and him."

Suddenly Mary hit her fist on the table and said: "I knew from the beginning that he could not be trusted. It's just as well he did not come," but Deborah answered: "It would be better if he had."

★★★

On Mondays Ruth did not have to work at the diner, Deborah had flexible hours at St. Francis, and Travis did not have to report for work at the Starlight until 4:00. Ruth had invited Deborah for lunch. At the end of the lunch Deborah said to Travis that she had missed him at the barbecue. Travis, who was always quick with answers, explained: "Well, I would have liked to have gone but I did not want to spoil it for all of you."

"What are you talking about?" Deborah asked.

"I have a strong feeling that since my adventure in Las Vegas, your parents no longer care much for me. I am sure that they were hoping that I would not come along."

"And I am certain that they were hoping that you *would* come along," answered Deborah.

"Let's let bygones be bygones," said Ruth. "We have coffee and pumpkin pie for dessert." Pouring the coffee, Ruth added: "I don't know about you, but lately I have preferred honey instead of sugar in my coffee. Who wants some?"

"I happen to like it, too," said Deborah, but Travis remained silent and finally added: "No, I have gotten used to drinking it black."

Ruth went to get the honey, pretended to be looking in various places and came back empty-handed saying: "I am quite certain I had a small jar of honey, but I cannot find it any place."

"I'll bring you a couple of jars the next time I come," Deborah assured her while Travis drank his coffee quickly and explained that today he had to leave early in order to iron out a few problems with the owner of the Starlight. "Save me a piece of the pie for tonight." Within a few minutes he was out the door. Ruth yelled after him: "The hell with the owner of the Starlight. Leave him and get a better paying job!"

The Pontiac pulled off the driveway. It was not headed south in the direction of the Starlight but north. Ruth remarked that lately he had frequently left for work at this hour and always been rather secretive about it.

"Do you still think a lot about Ernie?" asked Deborah.

"Ernie? Yes, I do. Ernie was timid and indecisive, sometimes still a little boy, but there is no doubt that he loved me with his whole heart. He was very sincere. He and his friend Chip did beautiful work together with painting and hanging wallpaper. Ernie could have become a fine interior decorator if he had taken courses in that field. He was kind of an artist. You should see the wonderful job he did in Larry's house next door!"

"How about if we paid Ernie a visit at the cemetery?" Deborah's question was more like a suggestion.

"I would love to."

"And I would not mind visiting Isabel's grave. I haven't been there since her funeral. She was a very misguided person with an alcohol and a cigarette problem, but deep down she had a warm heart, I think. Let's go and say a prayer for her." Ruth cleared the table and Deborah went to retrieve her cane which she had left in the bathroom.

It was a twenty-minute walk north to the cemetery. Deborah was contemplating aloud: "Autumn has arrived but here in this part of the world one can hardly tell the difference between summer and autumn. I would like to live where the green leaves of the trees turn golden yellow, red and maroon."

"Yes," answered Ruth, "but I like it also where I don't have to cover the roses from November to April. Tell me something: Do you think that the dead know what we are doing? Do they hear us as we talk to them? Can there be communication?"

"I am certain of that because in reality they are not dead. Only their former bodies are dead. I am also convinced that our grandparents, all of our relatives and friends up there, take an interest in what we are doing. In other words, if we talk to Isabel and Ernie, they know that we are talking to them."

"How do you know?"

"My gut feeling tells me. By themselves they probably could not, but because they enjoy the beatific vision, they know things through God. Heaven presupposes perfect happiness. How could there be perfect happiness if you were completely cut off from your children? Besides that: I do not think that the Holy Spirit would allow the church to lead us for centuries into believing that we can ask the saints to intercede for us if there were no communication. If the saints can hear us, so can everyone in heaven, because everyone in heaven is a saint. That the church and the pope single out certain ones and declare that they are saints makes no difference. I talk to all of them."

"It's mind boggling if you think about it," said Ruth. "Do you like walking through cemeteries?"

"I do," answered Deborah, "because it makes me feel close to them. From a rational viewpoint it makes little sense because our friends are not where their bones are deteriorating, but for me it becomes an emotional matter. Whether I see a photo of a departed friend or his or her tombstone, an emotional line of communication becomes established. When I go to a historical museum and stand in front of a statue of President Lincoln, I know that he is not there physically, but emotionally it places me into his time and his presence."

They had reached the cemetery. It was landscaped like a park with trees, bushes, green spaces and potted flowers on some of the graves.

Deborah was still theologizing when Ruth pulled her by the arm and said: "Look, there is someone at Isabel's grave."

"No, that can't be!"

"Quiet, Debbie!"

They tiptoed toward the grave and clearly recognized Travis. "Travis not at the Starlight but at her grave? I can't believe it," whispered Ruth.

"You don't have to believe it. You can see it."

Finally they were in earshot of him but hid behind a dense bush. Travis kept moving from one side of the grave to the other and most of what he was saying they could not make out except for one sentence: "I am tired of being compared to him. I am much too nice a guy. I should have put a match to his beehives, ... the way they gossip about you and me .... Isabel, I am so sorry for not having visited you more often during your final weeks, but ...." The rest was carried away by the shifting wind.

Ruth debated whether she should walk up to him and confront him but Deborah urged that they should sneak out as quietly as they had come in because she could see him throw a tantrum if he found out that they had been listening in on him. He would never ever trust them again. "Let's come back some other time," she suggested.

On the way home Deborah said: "At least he believes that he can communicate with the dead," and all Ruth could answer to that was to giggle. She felt relieved because now she knew that Eric was innocent. But then she very seriously asked:

"Wouldn't it be better if Travis knew that he had given himself away?"

"Maybe, Ruth, but it would totally destroy your patched-up marriage."

"Debbie, I am at a loss. He seemed to be a changed man who was trying to blend in again. He had me convinced that he was ready for a new start. What makes that man flip-flop?"

"Ruth, no psychiatrist knows all about the human brain's chemistry. Only God does."

ON A ROLLER COASTER

The day after Ruth and Deborah had observed Travis at Isabel's grave, Ruth was waitressing at the diner. After the lunch crowd had left, the phone rang. The owner of the restaurant waved at Ruth and yelled: "It's for you, Mrs. Riley."

Inspector Haberdink was on the phone. He had the lab results and said: "Mrs. Riley, only the fingerprints on the glass which you had marked with a T were found on the pie tin, together with those of your father. The prints on the glass that you had marked with an E did not match those on the pie tin. That your father's prints were on the pie tin was to be expected because he said that he had picked it up and thrown it into the bee house."

Mr. Haberdink, I thank you for taking care of this. I would like to retrieve those two water glasses on my way home from work today, shortly after 4:00 if that's okay."

"Mrs. Riley, I am afraid that will have to wait. Since we may be dealing with a crime, the Chief of Police would like for you to stop in at your earliest convenience to let him know what the letters E and T stand for. For the time being the two water glasses will be kept pending a criminal investigation. I trust that your dad got rid of all of the honey that was in the six hives."

"He did, Mr. Haberdink."

Ruth was now in a panic. What if Travis found out what she had done? Neither she nor her dad had any intention to prosecute. All she wanted was clarification. On the other hand, a burden had been lifted off her because Eric's innocence had now been firmly established. *Poor Eric! I am so sorry I had to put you through all of this.*

On her way home, Ruth was filled with dread having to face Travis after midnight when he would come home from work. *A face-to-face conversation seems unavoidable. On the other hand, why not simply pretend that I don't know anything? I'll just act dumb and state that I no longer think that Eric had anything to do with it. If I told him about the water glasses, Travis would lose his cool. If only my parents will agree to the pretense of ignorance! I've got to talk to them first. I feel that fate is making me ride on a roller coaster.*

Instead of stopping at the police station on the way home, Ruth talked to her parents and expressed her frustration. Luckily, both agreed that under the circumstances it would be best not to let on to Travis what they now knew. When Ruth came home she took Eric aside, hugged him and told him that he was not the bee killer. She also told him how difficult and hard it had been for her to suspect him but that several facts had pointed in his direction. Angie listening in the doorway breathed a sigh of relief.

"Who did it?" she asked.

Ruth simply answered that the police were still investigating.

"Do I now get my slingshot back?" asked Eric.

"Yes, you will get it back. Angie, do you know where it is?"

It took her no more than a minute to retrieve it from her room. When Eric examined it he seemed a little disappointed. It no longer looked to him as pretty and as big as he thought it had been some time ago. Obviously, missing it for what had seemed to be an eternity, his imagination had idealized and magnified it.

"Dad promised that he would make me a real nice one. This one looks so small and crummy. I knew I didn't do it. Did the police say who did?"

After a while Ruth answered: "No, they are still investigating."

Ruth stayed up until 2:30 in the morning, praying and thinking about what to say to Travis, but finally she dozed off in the reclining chair. Suddenly she heard a noise at the back door but nobody was there.

It must have been the wind rattling at the screen door that Travis promised to fix a long time ago. She decided to go to bed, but first she called the Starlight to find out from him at what time he intended to come home. The man who answered, apparently the owner, told her that Travis had not shown up for work that afternoon but that earlier in the day he had asked for his pay one day in advance saying that he needed it for some urgent work on his Pontiac.

By now it was 3:00 a.m. and Ruth decided to get three or four hours of sleep. She fell into bed like a sack of potatoes and within ten minutes was so sound asleep that she did not notice Travis tiptoeing into the room and carefully crawling into their bed. At 7:00 the alarm clock woke both of them and Ruth said that it was time to get breakfast ready for Angie and Eric and take them to school. She would, as always, go straight to the diner but come home after the lunch rush, around 3:00, and pick up the children on the way home. She kissed him *good bye* and said: "We need to talk." Kissing him, she smelled a perfume that was definitely not hers.

That evening she again waited for him, but at midnight she decided to call it quits. She had not been to the bedroom since coming home from work. But what was that? His dresser drawers were half open and mostly empty. Most of his shirts and several of his suits and shoes were gone. On her pillow Ruth found a note which read:

> Ruth, thanks for spying on me. With the water glasses you effectively destroyed our marriage. Give the children a hug and tell them that it is from me. Also tell them not to worry about me. I will be in touch some day, but for now, don't bother looking for me.
>
> Travis

"My fate," Ruth said and her face turned pale. She became haunted by guilt feelings, and wracking her brain over the question how Travis could have found out about the water glasses, she could not get any sleep that morning.

After breakfast Angie and Eric wondered where dad was. He rarely had breakfast with them. Because of his work schedule he had gotten into the habit of sleeping in late. Before taking off for school the kids would, however, peek into his bedroom and yell: "Bye Dad." Ruth, not wanting to spoil the school day for them, told them that he had had to leave early, which wasn't exactly a lie, she thought. Later that morning, while the two were in school, Ruth, emotionally exhausted, called the diner saying that she was sick and went to see her parents again to break the news to them.

Ruth sounded panicky when she said: "I cannot for the world figure out how Travis discovered the secret with the water glasses. Fred turned slightly pale and said: "A few says ago Haberdink told me that he had taken the water glasses and the pie tin to the police lab for analysis. Later I went to the police station to see if the results were in. They had not yet come in, but one of the police officers who had been to the lab was curious to know what the letters E and T stood for, and I told him."

"How could you do that?" asked Mary. "He may have told others who frequent the Starlight or who associate with Travis in some other way. Travis may have been tipped off about the results, even before Haberdink knew them."

"I'm sorry," said Fred as he looked down. "At the time these possibilities did not occur to me. I am not clairvoyant." He earned a dirty look from Mary when a little later he stated that he had no intention of suing Travis.

"Why not?" Mary asked.

"It would only make things worse between him and Ruth and between him and us. The bees have been saved. Let's forget the whole thing. If the police want to investigate, fine, but I think that we should forgive and forget. The less we see of him the better."

"Forgive?" shouted Mary. "You must have lost your marbles!"

"Mom, Dad means *forgive*. *Forget* is something else. Don't let my husband's impulsive crime ruin your marriage as well. I agree with Dad. The less we see of him from now on the better. Angie and Eric might disagree with that. They still love him." Mary predicted: "Some day, they, too, will realize that it was he who abandoned them twice."

"Yes, some day. But what about now? What am I to tell them now?" Ruth sounded desperate.

"It's tough," whispered Fred. "We ought to consult Debbie on that. She often comes up with workable suggestions in tricky situations. In the end, however, the burden falls on your shoulders. It's your fate and I don't envy you. If you and Debbie can think of something we can do, don't hesitate to say it."

Trying to help, Mary added: "Right now the children need to be convinced that you love them."

"I am not going to work today. l called in sick. I need time to think things through." Ruth stayed for lunch and decided to swing by St. Francis on the way home.

★★★

Before supper, as Angie was doing her homework, Eric came to her bedroom.

"Angie, Dad's gone. He left."

"I know. If only I knew why! Mom said that she isn't sure why. She said that Larry next door told someone that a policeman had told someone at the Starlight that Dad may have poisoned the bees."

"I don't believe it. Mom once told us that there are a lot of gossipers in this town. It's always '*told someone … told someone.*'"

"I don't believe it either. Why would he do a thing like that? I wanted to ask Mom this morning before school, but she seemed to be crying, so I didn't."

"Mom was crying?" Eric sounded surprised. "I have never seen her cry."

"Of course not. When handling a tough boy like you, she must be tough and not cry."

"Wait a minute. You are no angel either."

"I am just teasing, Eric. In this town, if someone hears a rumor he adds something to it when telling it to someone else, and before you know it, the story has changed and the rumor has become a crime. I hate this town. Maybe, Las Vegas wasn't such a bad idea."

"First it was me, now it's Dad. I bet you he went back to Las Vegas to finish the project he was working on."

"I don't know. He would have told us and not just snuck out without saying goodbye. I am not looking forward to school tomorrow, especially recess."

"Me neither," added Eric.

MÉLISSA

What is it about humans? Their minds are so complicated. There is so much tension between them. We can feel their tension. In wanting to hurt each other they sometimes end up hurting us, and knowingly so. It is hard to imagine the pain that our cousins must have suffered when ingesting and storing poisoned honey.

Our brains are no more than one fourth of a cubic millimeter in size. It would take about 700,000 bee brains to make one human brain. Humans, therefore, ought to be 700,000 times more intelligent than we are, but in the bee world we all know that they are not. In other words, a big brain is just a big brain, nothing more.

When bees fight, it is in self-defense. When they sting a human, it is in self-defense. When humans sting each other, the cause is hatred or greed or just poor judgment, which is just another word for "dumb." At the bottom of hatred lie ignorance and misunderstanding. It shows that knowledge and understanding are not in proportion to the size of the brain. Poor judgment? It shows that common sense is not in proportion to the size of the brain either. God, I thank you for having created us as bees.

A BEACON OF LIGHT

After talking to Deborah on her way home from work, Ruth felt a little better. Her fate, however, dampened Deborah's enthusiastic spirit because other people's problems always became her problems. She felt that her fate in life was minimal compared to Ruth's. Nevertheless, even at St. Francis she was not immune to disappointments. There was the case of Mrs. Fehling. She had died of a heart attack, and her children blamed Deborah for it arguing that she had greatly upset their mother with her talking about heaven and hell. "We are convinced," they said to Sr. Mary Louise, "that that strange woman upset our mother with her hellfire preaching and thus provoked the heart attack."

Even though Sr. Mary Louise answered that Miss Walsh never ever engaged in any sort of hellfire preaching but rather the opposite, Mrs. Fehling's son stated that he would contact their lawyer.

It wasn't only outsiders who created problems. At times one or the other staff member became jealous of Deborah's success when their attempts at calming down a patient had failed while Deborah subsequently succeeded. Sometimes, that resulted in bad-mouthing Miss Walsh. It was after days like those that one could find Deborah sitting by herself in the sisters' private chapel. The stained glass window behind and above the altar with its modern art design and its deep red, green, blue, and purple colors, which lent themselves to various subjective interpretations, let her mind wander from setbacks into new directions, even into the bliss of heaven. That, however, would not make the reality of the slanders disappear. It only made her feel closer to Jesus Christ in whose real presence in or with the consecrated bread in the tabernacle behind the altar she firmly believed and which gave her the optimism to move on.

One day, Sr. Mary Louise invited Deborah to the sisters' private community room with an adjacent little library. On the bulletin board of the library she showed Deborah a large photo with three young women looking at a painting. One could clearly recognize it as "Christina's World" by Andrew Wyeth. They were wearing neat identical dresses and white veils which were different from the Franciscan habits of the sisters. That type of an outfit very much appealed to Deborah's fine sense of aesthetics. Mary Louis explained that these young ladies were novices at the motherhouse and that she hoped that after completion of their novitiate at least one of them would be assigned to St. Francis. Whether it was the three novices' interest in the painting or their attractive outfits that made Deborah go back to the photo several times was not clear, but it gave Sr. Mary Louise, who only pretended to be reading the newspaper, proof that God works in mysterious ways.

"How would you like to come with me to the motherhouse this weekend?" she asked Deborah after a while. "You could get to know these young women and let me know what you think of them. Would one of them be cut out for work at St. Francis? I trust your common sense."

Deborah did not know what was happening to her. She never got invited and now she was even asked for her input. She could not know that Mary Louise knew the three novices and their qualifications quite well already.

"Of course, I would love to come along."

"How about Sunday morning at 8:30? I'll drive. That would give us enough time to attend their 10 o'clock mass and time to show you around before lunch. After lunch you could spend time with the young ladies."

"That would be just fine. Thank you so much, sister. I don't know what to say."

"You already said it. Don't be late. Bye, Miss Walsh."

"Bye, sister."

On the way home Deborah nearly missed a stop sign while a cop was waiting just around the bend.

★★★

The cleanliness of the motherhouse impressed Deborah. She had never seen such shiny hallway floors. During Mass, the celebrant was the only man around the altar. All the others were women. As long as the celebrant kept quiet, – and he was the kind who did, -- there would be no repercussion from the bishop concerning females as altar girls, lectors, and even Eucharistic ministers.

During dinner with the candidates and novices, Deborah began to feel like part of the family. Nobody stared at her. She never had the feeling that she was different. After dinner the novices worked in the kitchen and Deborah decided to pitch right in, invited or not. Then, accidentally, she dropped one of the finer glass dishes, which shattered into a dozen pieces on the floor. Only once within the last few years had she felt more embarrassed than now, and that event now rushed through her memory like a rewound film. In one of her English classes she had been turned on to poetry and one of her classmates let her borrow the poems which she had written in a decorative notebook. If there had been grades for penmanship on the college level, that girl would have had the only A in class. Her intention was to have the poems published some day. Well, inadvertently, Deborah left that beautiful book of poems on the bus seat on her way home from the university, and eight frantic phone calls to the bus company yielded no results. When the classmate told Deborah that she had no copy of many of those poems, both felt devastated. *Lost forever,* she thought as the young ladies swept up the pieces of glass. *How clumsy of me and how careless of the poet for not keeping a copy in a safe place!*

"I am so sorry," she whispered to the candidates and the novices.

"Now you are one of us," said a husky looking novice who was from Austria. "At home we say: *Scherben bringen Glück.*" Then one of them translated: *"Broken crockery brings you luck".*

"That's what we say in the Alps. Therefore it must be true," added the Austrian.

After dinner the novices had their daily conference with the novice mistress and Deborah decided to take a walk in the park behind the convent. The footpath led alongside a little fruit orchard, a row of oleanders, and partially shaded rhododendrons, where a little forest began. Deborah followed the narrow footpath into the forest. It led to a gazebo where two sisters were engaged in a lively conversation. Being too shy and polite to intrude, Deborah sat on a rock at a safe distance but close enough to follow most of the conversation.

"… ordination may not be the best way for women to make a difference," she heard one of them say. Her ears popped up.

"Why is that? At our last retreat I got the impression that you were one of the critics who thought that ordination for women was long overdue. You said that one of the reasons for problems in the church is that it is run by men only."

"Yes, and I still believe that, but last week I visited some of my cousins who are Episcopalians. I assume you know that I am a convert. Their new women priests, few in number, are frequently given positions with little income, positions in small congregations that nobody wants except for retired clergy who wish to stay with one foot in the profession, or who just want to help out. They work their tails off. Female Associate Pastors are often assigned to tasks in the parish where you are damned if you do and damned if you don't, or they are given most of the wakes and funerals. I have heard similar complaints from female ministers in several Protestant churches. Many of these women are in but not equal."

"It's a beginning but it stinks."

"It certainly does. But then there are also those who hold normal positions. They are fully accepted but it is precisely some of them who create a problem. They look down on conservative women who do not believe in women ordination. That does not help the cause either. That is just as bad as when career oriented women wrinkle their noses at those who find fulfillment in devoting themselves to family, house and garden. Some of the male clergy discriminate against the progressive women and some of the female clergy belittle the traditional women. Some of the female clergy are just as high nosed as their male counterparts."

"That problem is not confined to the clergy. I have several nieces who look down on classmates who dream of having children and devoting themselves to family and home. One of them is a business major who cannot understand why a talented young woman would want to major in home economics. We live in sick times. ... Also don't forget that this whole issue of women's ordination is a new movement in the Protestant churches. These are only the early Seventies. Wrinkles need to be ironed out. In our church it hasn't even started yet."

"I am afraid that we may not see it in our lifetime, but let us hope that when the time comes, the Catholic Church will have learned something from the Protestant experience."

Deborah could not make out the rest of the conversation. What she had heard, however, disturbed her and she decided to walk back to the convent and spend some time in the chapel. She needed to ask God a few tough questions and sort out things in her head.

At suppertime the sisters made her feel like one of them again and even called her Debbie. On the way home that evening Debbie expressed her sincere appreciation for having been invited to visit the motherhouse. As Sr. Mary Louise dropped her off, Deborah said to her: "You know, for being Mother Superior and the director of a large nursing home, you are easy to talk to."

"Debbie, I firmly believe that open ears, reading people's minds, and respect are the prerequisites for getting to the heart of a person." The car was gone before Deborah could think of a meaningful answer. *So that is how she got to me and kept me in her grip.*

★★★

Monday morning Deborah was waltzing around Ruth's living room like a hyper fifth grader.

"What has gotten into you, Debbie?"

"I had a most wonderful experience."

"What could that be?"

"Well, I spent Sunday at the motherhouse of the Franciscans. Sr. Mary Louise invited and introduced me, and you know what? That is the most wonderful bunch of women in any place."

"Girl, are you hyper! Lunch is almost ready. Come to the kitchen before you knock down one of my flower vases. What do you have in that bag?"

"A bottle of Burgundy to celebrate the occasion."

"Celebrate what?"

"Oh, you should have seen that nun drive. My hands were sweating. She must have been a race car driver before joining the order."

"Is that what we are celebrating?"

"No, sit down so you won't faint. I may have found my vocation. I'll apply to be a Franciscan."

"YOU, a nun? You with your liberal views in theology? You are pulling my leg."

"No. I'm not. You'd be surprised to hear the viewpoints of some of them. I'll blend right in with that group."

"In other words, you found acceptance. Does that also mean that you have been accepted?"

"Sr. Mary Louise appreciates what I do and she seems to like me. She is going to finagle it. This will be a new life experience for me."

"I am sure that she did some fast talking, and I hope that she did not do a snow job on you. What about your dreams for ordination? Are they out the window?"

"Not entirely. The novice mistress of all people seemed to agree with me when I stated that the elimination of women from ordination constitutes discrimination and injustice within the church. All I wanted was to make clear that she knew where I stood on this, regardless of consequences. Was I in for a surprise when she said: 'The church wants to work for justice around the world, which she should, but justice should begin at home.'"

Ruth poured the Burgundy into crystal wine glasses, which were a wedding present from her parents. "Congratulations, Sister Debbie. Here is to your future."

"Thanks Ruth, to *our* future. Oh, any word from Travis?"

"None. Dad told me again that he had decided not to pursue the case with legal action in spite of pressure from the Beekeepers Association. He wants to let bygones be bygones. Should he ever meet Travis again, he will pretend that guilt has not been proven."

"Now that takes the attitude of a saint."

"Travis's sudden escape, however, proves his guilt," said Ruth.

"I know it does, Ruth, but who knows how the molecules of the brain interact and what kind of tricks they can play on the human mind, its logic, its reaction? I am saying this because what Travis did is so contrary to his character. -- Now, to go back to the topic from before: Realistically and practically, ordination is out for me, whether it be in our church or in one of the Protestant Churches. It's a phantom in my life, but the ministry which I can perform, is no phantom, it's reality."

"Are you sure they will accept you?"

"I don't have it in writing, but the impression I got from Sister Marie Louise was that I could possibly move in next month, November 1."

"On All Saints Day. How fitting! I think, however, that you'll be a bit of a devilish nun, a little devil among the saints."

In answer to that Deborah's smile reached almost from ear to ear. After a sip of the wine, she said: "First I'll be a candidate, then a novice, and finally a devilish sister. I like the new habits the younger ones wear."

"I feel relieved to hear that there is a group that appreciates and accepts you, a group that you like as well. I really mean that."

"I know that you mean that. You have always been straight-forward. I haven't told Mom and Dad yet."

"Now be realistic! November 1 has not yet been decided. Nothing has."

"You should come and see that place. Their church is a modern structure with stained glass windows all around. The colors and designs are intoxicating."

"What do they show?"

"That is up to each spectator's imagination, and that is what I like about modern church windows."

"You certainly have some unique icons in your head. Beech trees, bees, church windows …"

"Don't forget oak trees."

After lunch the two took a look at Ruth's last roses. Ruth clipped the nicest ones for Deborah to take home. Before they parted Deborah asked: "You know what inspired me most about that place?"

"What?"

"The entire time that I was there nobody stared at me. Do you remember what Mrs. Jones down the street once said to us? She said that she had never been really aware of being black until she moved into our neighborhood. We grew up and we live on the outskirts of an upper class community of snobs. One week after Mrs. Jones' family had moved into one of the streets here, three FOR SALE signs appeared on the front lawns. I know what it feels like to be stared at."

It was time for Ruth to pick up the children. On afternoons when Ruth had to work the children would walk home. On the way to school Ruth prayed: *God, watch over Debbie and let it last. But what about the children and me? Do you have a solution for us us as well?"*

Deborah had similar thoughts as she limped along the gravel road home: *Who is the one with no help in sight? Not I. What is she going to tell the kids?*

★★★

One evening the doorbell rang while Deborah was alone at home. It was Edith, and no sooner was she in the house when, with a sound of bewilderment, she asked: "What is all that I hear about, you, Debbie? Are you entering a convent? Are you on drugs?"

"Edith, calm down! Why does this decision bother you? It will not interfere with our friendship."

"I don't understand how someone in her right mind would want to be locked up in a cloister. What has become of your plans for the ministry?"

"Now wait a minute. You are the one who told me that one could also function as a minister without being ordained. That is precisely what I am doing now and what I will be doing as a Franciscan. Those Franciscan sisters I work with are not at all 'locked up in a cloister.' They teach. They do social work. They console. They inspire."

"They inspired you alright."

"Two Mormon missionaries once told me that God has a plan for all of us, even for a scarecrow like me. It took me a while to realize that, and then it took me a while to accept it. The desire to be ordained is still there and it will never leave me. You even find it among some of the sisters and, believe it or not, among some of the older ones who make no bones about it. I blend right in. At the same time, we feel that we are needed where we are, and we believe *that* to be our calling."

"I give up," replied Edith, but I would like to visit you at your place of work and watch those friends of yours. Nuns have always seemed distant to me. I have never conversed with any of them. I am open to see and learn. You are either right or you have been brainwashed."

"Don't forget that I am nine years older than you with a little more life experience. I also make better coffee than you do. Come, let's go and have some, it's decaf."

As they were sipping decaffeinated coffee, Deborah said: "I am looking forward to your visits. Be assured that whatever your conclusions may be at the end, it will not impact on our friendship, you in a business suit or in a maternity dress, I in a Franciscan sisters' outfit. We'll make a wonderful pair."

Edith raised her cup and said: "Let's drink to that."

★★★

Deborah had just helped Old Jimmy in 210 with his lunch. It had become an almost daily routine. On account of Jimmy's slow chewing and swallowing it frequently cut into Deborah's own lunch hour, but Jimmy was always very appreciative. At the sight of Deborah he always emerged from his usual state of psychological depression. That in Deborah's mind made up for the loss of part of her lunch hour. When she left the room while Jimmy was still looking out the window and talking, she saw Leicester coming out of his mother's room down the hall. That makes my day, she thought. He must have taken me seriously at the wedding the weekend before last. She whistled to catch his attention. After a short greeting she said to him: "This is still part of my lunch hour. Let's go to the cafeteria and I'll get you a complimentary cup of coffee like in the good old days at Santa Clara."

"Nice room," he commented, after she brought the cups to a table at a window.

"This is where the ambulatory retirees eat. It would be better if your mother ate here but she prefers to eat in her room. It makes me happy to see you visit her."

"Tell me something, Deborah. On the day of the wedding, how did you know that she was my mother?"

"She once told me bits and pieces of her life's story and that she had a son at Santa Clara. When she mentioned the name Leicester, I put two and two together."

"She gave me a lecture about going to church. I appeased her by saying: 'Mom, don't worry too much. I pray to Jesus. He is like a brother to me." That made her happy."

"Leicester, was that the truth?"

"Yeah, sometimes I really do, especially before exams."

"Before exams … hm. Let's suppose that you had helped someone who had asked you for help in a time of need. A week later you met him in the street and he did not even say 'hi' to you. How would you feel?"

"I would feel pissed off. Why are you bringing that up? It never happened."

"Yes, it did. You ask God to help you before and during exams, but a week later you no longer talk to him. He must feel pissed off to use your expression."

"Now you have pushed me into a corner again. I thought that we were going to have a friendly conversation. I wish you would stop preaching to me. It's annoying."

"You are right. I have to stop doing that. It is sufficient that your mother preaches to you. By the way, you never told me how you fared with that essay about the Mater Dolorosa sculpture."

"He liked it, gave me a B, thanks to you."

"I'm happy to hear that."

"On the back of the picture a pious soul ad written the words: *Mary, our mother.* That made no sense to me. She was Jesus' mother, not our mother."

"Now wait a minute. You just told your mother that Jesus was like a brother to you. That makes Mary your mother."

"Darned, there you cornered me again. You are too smart for being a woman. No wonder you graduated *summa cum laude.*

"There are a lot of smart women. It's about time you men accepted that fact. If you had married Edith, -- you told me how fond you were of her, -- you would have ended up with a real smart one."

"I would know how to handle her. I bet you she knows nothing about baseball and football. What was his name again?"

"Elvis."

"Elvis, yes. He looked a little wild. That doesn't go with her looks.

"Yes, he did. His deportment is not nearly as refined as hers, and his wind-blown hair looked like that of a bushman, but he was an almost straight 'A' student. In that sense the two are a good match." "That does not mean that he is smart."

Since Deborah did not answer to that, Leicester remarked: "These are damn good cookies."

"Go ahead and finish them. I have to watch my figure. By the way, I hope that you won't mind my being so outspoken. I have become that way over the years, but I like you, especially now that you are visiting your mother. I hope to see you every week, twice a week would even be better. I am surrounded by a lot of doomsday faces here. Now and then I need someone I can tease."

"I don't mind you teasing me. I love to conversate with you."

"Converse. – I have to make my round now. Hope to see you soon."

"In a few days," said Leicester. As he left the entrance hall, Deborah heard him muttering the words "converse" and conversate.

DEATH IN A FLOPHOUSE

The owner of a flophouse in Las Vegas received a complaint by one of his tenants one morning. The tenant said that he had not been able to sleep all night because the guy next to him had had his TV on very loud since the day before. "The walls are not soundproof. I banged on the wall but that guy must be deaf."

"What is the room number?"

"14."

"Room 14. Let's see here. That is Mr. Riley. He seemed to be friendly when he checked in last week. Let's go and talk to him. If he does not lower the volume I'll kick him out."

The owner knocked on the door, three times. No answer. "He must be here because his car is out there." The owner unlocked the door and yelled "Mr. Riley!" Mr. Riley was lying fully dressed on his bed and seemed sound asleep, but stepping closer to him the two noticed that he was dead. They turned off the TV set. On the night table they found his wallet, his car keys, a half empty bottle of sleeping pills, and an empty whiskey flask. The owner called the police. One of the two police officers who had responded in no time, found a small plastic bag of cocaine, in Mr. Riley's lunch bag.

After the coroner had picked up the body, the police department called Ruth whose phone number and address were in Mr. Riley's wallet.

"Mrs. Riley?"

"Yes."

"Mrs. Riley, this is the Las Vegas Police Department. Do you have a husband by the name of Travis?"

"Yes."

"I am afraid we have very bad news for you. Your husband was found dead this morning in his bed at a rooming house." ... There was silence. ...

"Mrs. Riley, are you still on the line?"

"Yes, I am."

"I am so sorry to have to ask you a few questions at a time like this. "Was your husband into drugs?"

"No, he was not. That would be news to me."

"We found cocaine in his lunch bag. He also had an empty flask of whisky and a bottle of sleeping pills on his night table." The pill bottle was half empty."

"He never took any kind of drugs to my knowledge, not even sleeping pills. He did drink whisky. He was employed at a night club."

"An autopsy report will tell us the cause of death. We will keep you informed. In the meantime, either you or another close relative will have to come here to identify the body and retrieve his personal belongings, including the car."

"Officer, his parents live in Los Angeles. It would be easier for them to drive to Las Vegas than for me," Ruth explained.

"That is entirely up to you folks. Why don't you talk to them, give them the bad news and decide? Call us back. We will have the exact address of our police department for you." One of us will then take that person to the morgue."

Ruth gave the police officer the address and phone number of her in-laws but told him that she would call them. Afterwards, Ruth sat in Travis' rocking chair and cried. *Has my constant nagging about finding a better paying job driven him to selling drugs? Has lack of success and embarrassment over what he did driven him to end it all? Was I part of the problem?*

That night Fred flew from San Francisco to Las Vegas and Bill, Travis's dad, drove from Los Angeles. Bill had tears rolling down his cheeks as the undertaker pulled back the cover sheet. The report from the coroner arrived the next morning at the police department. They called Fred and Bill in the hotel room which they shared. No traces of cocaine had been found in Travis's body, and the assumption of the police was that he had been selling drugs. The report also revealed that Travis had died of an overdose of sleeping pills and whisky.

Bill and Fred agreed that the thing to do would be a quiet church service in either Los Angeles or Mountain View, followed by cremation, but that Ruth should have the final say about that. Ruth then decided to have the body shipped to her. Fred and Bill split the cost of the transfer.

Fred drove Travis's Pontiac back to Mountain View because Ruth was co-owner. At a rest stop on that long trip Fred looked for a flashlight in the Pontiac's glove compartment. There he spotted a small leather bag which contained a tiny, beautifully decorated jewelry box. In it he found a diamond ring. He thought first that he was having a vision. On the inside of the ring one could clearly read the engraved date 5-1-1940.

★★★

Breaking the news to the children was not easy, but they remained amazingly calm. In the morning Angie entered Eric's bedroom and said: "Eric, Mom suggested that we should think of something that she could put into dad's casket before they bury him in the cemetery. Something like a farewell present."

"I wish I had something to give him." Eric sounded depressed.

"I know what, Eric. Let's write him a nice letter. We can tell him that we miss him and that we love him. We can also ask him not to forget us up there in heaven."

"You write the letter. You are good at that. You have written at least a hundred."

"Eric, I think that you should write your own, a little one."

Eric sat down at his table with a piece of stationery, but then he thought that whatever he could write would sound stupid compared to his sister's letter. So he went to his toy box to find something that he could give to Dad. Might he like a little jeep or a fighter plane? He had served in the Air Force in Korea. But then he thought that Mom and Angie would disapprove because they hated wars. He sat on his bed for a long time and suddenly it went like a flash through his head: The slingshot. With a cheerful glee he ran to Ruth and told her that he wanted to give Dad his slingshot. Ruth was moved because she could see that it was coming from Eric's heart. "Eric, you are a good son," she said to him and hugged him. "I am sure that Dad will appreciate it." When she told Angie about Eric's present, Angie was also happy and said: "Good riddance."

Instead of a traditional wake, only Travis's and Ruth's parents, Ruth, Deborah, Angie, Eric and Larry from next door said goodbye to Travis in Ruth's sunroom where the casket stood. Before Bill and Fred closed the casket, Ruth and Angie placed their envelopes on Travis's pillow and Eric laid his slingshot by his Dad's hands. He would have given the contents of his entire piggy bank to find out what the two had written in their letters.

The funeral was kept simple. The Veterans of Foreign Wars had sent their representatives, and Travis' friends from the Starlight had also shown up. The priest said nice words of hope and consolation during the ceremony in the cemetery, never mentioning the suicide. Ruth and Deborah had been afraid that he would allude to it. The honor guard of VFW fired three salvos, played taps which were somewhat off tune, folded the national flag accurately, and presented it with stiff reverence to Ruth. Leaving the cemetery, Eric felt very honored when Ruth gave him the flag to carry. Deborah had to rush back to St. Francis. Fred and Mary invited the small group of mourners, which included a few

co-workers from the Starlight, to their house for refreshments. Bill and
Helen spent the night there. They watched the sunset from their porch.
Bill and Helen lacked such a wonderful opportunity from their house in
Los Angeles which was located in an area where the homes were built
much too close together like little match boxes with six foot wide front
yards and virtually no backyards. Travis, they said, had always dreamed
of a larger house before moving to Mountain View.

Ruth and the children stopped once more at the cemetery on the
way home. The grave was now closed and a few small but colorful
flower bouquets gave some warmth to the clay soil on the grave on this
rather crispy October afternoon. Isabel's grave was only a few rows over
to the West. The Starlight nightclub had laid a wreath at the foot of the
grave with the inscription on the wreath's band reading: *To our Loyal
Co-worker and Friend* Travis.

★★★

On a busy Saturday afternoon, the day after the funeral, the
receptionist at St. Francis handed Deborah a letter addressed to Deborah
Walsh. The envelope showed neither the sender's name nor his or her
address, but a Las Vegas postal cancellation dated two days before
Travis had died. The handwriting looked somewhat shaky like that of
a ninety-year old person.

Dear Debbie,   *11-25-1975*

     *I can imagine the puzzlement on your face when receiving a
letter from your brother-in-law. I am sending it to St. Francis because
I want neither my in-laws nor Ruth to see it.*
     *I was able to undo the two contracts I had signed some time ago
for the remodeling of an old pawnshop into a sparkling nightclub.
Because the remodeling job had already been in process for a week,
I forfeited my down payments that I had hoped to get back. Now*

I am flat broke but have a dump of an unsellable pawnshop on my hands forcing me into some moneymaking activity which is not altogether kosher. That is not going well either. I may have to sell my old Pontiac.

Worse than that, psychologically I am down in the dumps and see no way out.

If Ruth had cooperated we could have a great future here in Vegas, but she calls this a "sin city." In spite of the fact that my in-laws never fully accepted me, and in spite of the fact that I have always been compared to your stepfather as an underachiever, I had adjusted to the idea of patching up my marriage until Ruth undertook that mean and disgusting step of having my water glass examined by the police to get my finger prints. What kind of a wife does that to her husband? That smells of legal actions. She had already shown disregard for my personal dignity when she expected me to become a janitor at a local school where everybody knew me, or a dishwasher in a restaurant, jobs for illegal aliens. Then I would certainly have been compared to your stepfather.

Debbie, you are different from them, and we have always been on good terms. More than once did I defend you before Isabel. Am I a "proud snob," a title your stepmother once gave me? I love my children, and that makes it impossible for me to sleep at night. Yes, I went overboard. I acted in anger, but I feel somewhat justified in what I did. Frustration, feelings of embarrassment, humiliation, envy, and anger drove me to what I did. Now they are driving me to booze and sleeping pills. What use is there for me to go on?

Please, tell Angie and Eric that I love them.

Down in the dumps,
Travis

After reading the letter, Deborah drove slowly because she felt the need to answer Travis.

"Travis, Travis. Why? Yes, we always got along well. I could and would have come to Las Vegas to talk to you and be with you for a day or two, had we only known where you were and had I only known what state of mind you were in. I understand your relationship problems with my parents and I feel for you. I must tell you, however, that you lacked control over your emotions and that you showed poor judgment at various times. Otherwise your Vegas dream would not have blinded you. No bank in this world would have loaned you the money needed to convert on old pawnshop into an elegant nightclub, and you would have realized that the revenge that you decided on for your in-laws by far exceeded what you considered humiliating comments. A little humility would have let you accept a low-level job that would have been temporary to begin with for the sake of Angie and Eric. Naiveté, pride, jealousy, and a little lack of honesty and openness did you in.

"Yes, Ruth taking your water glass to the police must have hurt your feelings, but what other way was there to prove Eric's innocence? And how do you think Ruth felt upon hearing that you were sharing a small apartment with a strip tease dancer and being kept in the dark about it?

In all fairness to you, however, I don't know how many sons-in-law in this world would have had the psychological strength and humility to face Ruth and my parents after the facts were on the table. Reconciliation may have been impossible, and so I do not condemn you for escaping."

Deborah had reached the cemetery that was on the way home. She stopped at Travis' grave, rearranged some of the flowers which the November wind had blown around and said: "Travis. Let's let bygones be bygones. I believe that you were not without good qualities that placated heaven. Please, help Ruth, Angie and Eric from above. They need you now more than ever."

The sky still radiated a light touch of red, pink and purple from the waning evening sun and cast its last shimmer on Travis' grave.

═══════ A CALL TO THE MINISTRY ═══════

Deborah was about to drive home after a busy day when Sister Mary Louise called her back inside and pulled her into her office. "Catching you is like running after a dog. You don't know how to walk. Sit down, please. A cup of tea before hitting the road?"

"Thank you. I would love it. As for walking, you are right. I never could, I only limp, but I limp like a young deer my family has often told me.

Sister had a thermos with hot water on her desk and an assortment of different teas. Deborah chose orange blossom tea.

"Tea is healthier for you than coffee," sister remarked.

"That's what my doctor and two young Mormon missionaries, wonderful people, have told me, but in my family everybody claims to be a coffee connoisseur."

Sister laughed. "I never was a coffee connoisseur but at your age I was a coffee addict and so was my dad. He drank at least six rather large mugs of the brew every day until he died of a heart attack. He was only 65. That's when I began to limit my coffee intake to one cup at breakfast time, no bulky mug but a dainty cup. With the many different kinds of tea on the market today, it is easy to wean yourself of coffee."

"Certainly something to think about," Deborah said after a while. "Tea might keep me from running. Do you know that you can make a deer sick by not allowing it to run?" The phone rang and sister could not answer to that. *The Mormons reject caffeine and alcohol altogether,* Deborah thought, and suddenly the kind and smiling face of Debbie the missionary surfaced in her imagination. The phone call ended too soon and when Deborah saw that sister's eyes were scrutinizing her, she pulled herself out of the past and said: "But Sister, you did not call me back inside to discuss the merits of tea. By the way, I like coffee but I am not addicted."

"I didn't think you were. There is something else I wanted to talk to you about. You have heard that Sr. Elinda has Parkinson's disease and she is at the point now where she can no longer be an extraordinary minister of the Eucharist. While Fr. Langan makes the rounds on Saturdays for those who are bedridden, he does not have the time to do so on other days. That is where Sr. Elinda came in. There are between 15 and 20 patients who wish to receive at least once during the week, more on Sundays. Would you like to perform that duty for the four weeks that we still have you here?

"I don't know what to say. Of course I would. That is something I have always dreamed of. It's almost like being a deacon."

"In that case consider yourself called to the ministry. You are in, young lady. Tomorrow, Saturday, Fr. Langan will give you some guidelines, some dos and some don'ts. You could just accompany him on his rounds tomorrow after mass around 10:30. Can you make it?"

"You bet I can."

"How about if you took Sundays and Wednesdays?"

"Sundays and Wednesdays are fine, and any other day on which you need someone." On the way home Deborah felt so overjoyed and eager to tell her parents that she almost ran over a squirrel.

★★★

Sunday came and Deborah was distributing communion, always finding a few inspiring words to say and praying with those who found it difficult or were no longer able to do so on their own. She felt that she was doing the job of a deacon. Why ordination? She also began to feel a little guilty at the thought that she was doing a better job talking to patients than her own pastor who had come to the house to pray with her dying grandfather, saying nothing but the Lord's prayer and a "Hail Mary. But then a certain guilt feeling overcame her, and in her mind she prayed: *God, don't let me start bragging now, because all of this is your work. You are just using me as your instrument, and that would indicate that you want me here, just as I am.*

While Deborah was on her way back to the chapel to return the leftover consecrated hosts to the tabernacle, Sr. Mary Louise and Sr. Elinda were having a cup of tea in Sr. Mary Louis's office. With the door open they saw Deborah limping at high speed along the corridor. "She is quite a woman," Sr. Marie Louise commented.

"In what sense?"

"She is bright and dedicated, has common sense, and sound progressive ideas."

"Progressive? Yes. Sound? I don't know. All that crap about women's ordination."

"I take the liberty to disagree with you there. I would have liked to see her become one of us."

"What's preventing it?"

"Our administration, the Provincial and her council."

"Any reason given?"

"No, none. All the Provincial was willing to state was that her council voted negatively. I am the one who has been asked to inform Miss Walsh because I am closest to her. I of all persons, I who talked her into it."

"I would not like to be in your shoes right now. I'll keep my fingers crossed."

"I appreciate that."

"I can think of two reasons in the minds of the council members.

"So can I. Her feelings will be hurt, but I believe that she is strong enough to accept it. I hate to lose her. She is ideal for this place."

DEBORAH

Deborah sat in the chapel at St. Francis. It was around suppertime and no one else was there at that hour. From the dining area one could hear the clatter of dishes. From the corner of her seat in the back of the chapel she had a great view of the windows on both sides. There was something special about those windows. With a little imagination these abstract works of art came to life. In the center, behind the tabernacle, a narrow but high window showed a tree as if it were growing out of the tabernacle. The walls of the chapel were shaped like two half circles and the color pattern of the windows alongside the walls suggested two mighty tree branches growing out of the trunk behind the tabernacle. Their green leaves stretched on both sides all the way to the back of the chapel. On both sides near the tabernacle the artist had chosen clear glass mixed in with yellow and orange colors as if the rays from the rising morning sun were shining through the green leaves. Toward the center of the sidewalls the colors between the green leaves gradually changed to blue indicating the blue sky at midday. Toward the end of the windows the stained glass changed to a rose color, then to a deep red with some interspersing of purple indicating the sky in the evening. The center and the origin of this mighty and ancient but healthy looking tree was the tabernacle from which it received its life and its strength. This tree reminded her of her favorite ancient beech tree.

The evening of my life is still at a distance, Lord Jesus. I am only 30. Mighty trees have always inspired me, but you are the real source of my inspiration. I firmly believe in Your presence here. I know that You read my deepest thoughts. You know that I felt like lightning had struck me after Sr. Mary Louise conveyed the decision to me. Afterwards I saw tears in her own eyes, but then I remembered my conversation with the two young Mormon missionaries. You are the one who created me as I am. Therefore, you must have a plan for my existence. There must be a purpose. First I thought that I had found it in a call to the ministry through ordination. Then it was a call to sisterhood, but You have given me indications that this here is the place where you want me.

The limitations of our human minds do not allow us to comprehend your plans and ways. Debbie, the Mormon missionary, was right when she kept saying that we should not try to meddle in Your plans. And yet, I am still upset about many of the successors to your apostles who are so set in their own ways that they are unwilling even to discuss certain changes in the church's structure. They are just as set in their old-fashioned minds as some of the Pharisees whom you scolded. They seem to be deaf. Don't let them close the windows that Pope John XXIII opened to let some fresh air into the church.

God, you are neither male nor female, neither black nor white, neither Asian nor Pacific Islander. Can you get that through their wrinkled brain linings? Becoming like one of us here on earth, you had to be born either male or female. Had you chosen to appear as the Daughter of God, I suppose that nobody would have listened to you 2000 years ago. Women had no place in public life. Today it would be different. Many countries have had women presidents, and some day, with your help, there will be female deacons, priests, and bishops. As for me, I thank you for helping me find my place in society. Having been denied admission to the seminary was, it seems, a blessing in disguise. I was a bit unrealistic in my dreams.

If I were delivering the most eloquent sermon wearing appealing vestments, some church goers might say: "How in the world did that scarecrow get up there?" Here at St. Francis I am effective, I am perceived as genuine. The persons I console know that I have been there. Dear God, please don't let my coworkers get jealous when they notice that Mrs. Wilber and others listen to me. Now I can even take communion to some of them, just like a deacon. And would I be here if I had a normal face and did not limp? Your ways are not our ways.

I dreamed two dreams. Fulfillment of anyone of those dreams might have given me financial security. But I'll be fine. I should learn from the bees. All they need and all they want are a comfortable, hollow space to build their combs in, water, nectar and pollen. All I really need is a room, big enough for a bed, a dresser, a bookcase, a desk and a chair … and a community which accepts me.

Dear God, who is the one who really needs your help? Ruth has it tougher than I ever did. She once said that she wants her children to have a positive memory of their dad. How is she going to do that? He was sweet on the surface. Isabel once told my mother that he thought highly of me. I think he really did. He also told friends that he had a good relationship with Ruth. That turned out to be barely skin deep. Gossipers will know more than Ruth herself. How can she shelter Angie and Eric from that? There is good in every person and only You know what tricks our brain's chemistry can play on us? I lie awake at night, just thinking about Ruth. She needs you now.

Deborah was suddenly shaken out of her meditations. Sr. Mary Louise was standing in the pew behind her tapping her on the shoulder and saying: "Young lady, I know that you are officially off work now but we have a new patient in room 115. Her relatives practically shoved her in here, kissed her goodbye, turned around and left. She keeps saying 'Why? Why are they taking me here? At home I have my room, my books. Why?' She seems beyond consolation. We need to make her feel welcome here."

"Okay, sister. I'll spend some time with her." *There goes one of my favorite TV programs at 7:30: "Mission Impossible" or "The Untouchables" with Eliot Ness.*

After Deborah dashed down the hallway, Sr. Mary Louise said to one of the nurses: "What a busy bee that woman is. She has a hard time walking, so she runs."

Postscript

My name is Mélissa. I'll come right out with it: You humans are a strange breed. In the animal world we act according to natural law. God made life easier for us honey bees. We don't have to ask, "Is this right?" or "Is this wrong?" We know it. We feel it. You humans, on the other hand, can make free decisions and when you do, your free decisions are not always based on rational thinking, on logic, or common sense. Often they are the result of emotional imbalances, which can be the cause for hatred, which in turn can result in unethical treatment of others, which then leads to guilt feelings that won't leave you alone. They have driven some people to suicide.

So many of you fear death. Are the guilt feelings one reason why you are afraid of dying? For me death was the most beautiful experience. It was like heaven. I wish I could go through it again.

In your world there is lack of communication resulting in misunderstandings. We communicate all the time in spite of our inability to speak the way you do. We use sign language and we understand each other. We are direct and to the point. We know neither envy nor hatred. When we fight or when we sting, we do it in self-defense and for survival.

Is it your free will that is doing you in? Why do you have a free will and we don't? Some of my sisters used to say that it was discrimination on the part of God. I am not so sure about that. You have been created in the image of God. Doesn't it say that in the story of the creation? "God created man in his image.

In the divine image he created him. Male and female he created them." That would explain free will. Because God is free, you are free.

In some ways, I guess, we too are created in His image. God is beautiful, and if you open your eyes you'll see that there is something very beautiful in every bee. Don't look at my face but at the faces of my siblings, perhaps under a magnifying glass, and you may find beauty, real beauty, and no makeup covering all sorts of blemishes. And, maybe, it is because God is all knowing, we too have an inborn desire to explore. How else would we survive? Maybe, it is because God is love that we all desire to love and to be loved. Have you ever watched young bees feeding babies and larvae? Do cats, dogs, and cows not lick their babies?

Would we have become envious of each other seeing Missi and Zimm fly faster than most of us? Would we resent the bumblebee, the butterfly, or even the wasp in our orange tree? You humans fight over territory, and resources. Some of you even steal from your own parents.

If you are created in the image of God, why don't you show it? If God is justice, you must have an inborn feeling for what is just and what is unjust. That being the case, why do you discriminate? It must be your free will, which is the culprit. You can want to discriminate, you can want to gossip behind someone's back. You can want to destroy someone's property.

I consider it a blessing in disguise that at the time of the creation we were discriminated against and do not have a free will. What might we have done to each other on a hot and muggy day in our bee box that was much too crowded?

Your free will makes you sway from one decision to another and, consequently, many of you have no sense of direction. Biologists marvel about our sense of direction. Rain or shine, we always find our way back to our families unless, of course, your insecticides alter our brains. Our sense of direction has become a timeless mystery.

Some of you worry day and night about your vocation. Half of you never find it and remain unfulfilled and unhappy over your daily chores. All we need is a little space, nectar, pollen and water to create a community.

You humans are a strange breed. Maybe, if you had five eyes as we do, you would see reality a little better, have a better sense of direction and you would be more like the Deborahs of old, and maybe, you would be nicer to us.

THE END

Lightning Source UK Ltd.
Milton Keynes UK
UKOW01f0435130416

272104UK00001B/115/P